Also by Michel Parry and
available from Redemption Books

Aggro

Countess Dracula

by Michel Parry

REDEMPTION
BOOKS

First published in the UK by Sphere Books, 1971.
This edition published by Redemption Books, 1995.
A divsion of Redemption Films Limited,
BCM PO Box 9235, London WC1N 3XX.

A catalogue record for this book is available from the
British Library.

ISBN 1 899634 00 2

Printed in the UK by
The Guernsey Press Company Limited.
Cover and photographic section printed by
Colin Clapp Printers.

Countess Dracula was inspired by a real person - a Transylvanian aristocrat of Hungarian origin, Countess Elizabeth Bathory (1560-1614).

Steeped in the cruelties of her turbulent age, Countess Elizabeth enjoyed lording it over her servants so much that she took to torturing and murdering the maids and other young females in her household.

Elizabeth must have created a considerable servant problem locally because at her trial in 1610 she was accused of murdering around 600 young women. It's been said that only when she turned her attentions to the daughters of the aristocracy were the authorities finally forced to take note of her activities and to act.

If the above figure is accurate, Elizabeth Bathory is the most prolific *female* serial killer known to history.

Elizabeth's interest in young women seems to have been largely sexually motivated Whether she seriously believed that bathing in the blood of virgins would help her retain her fading beauty can now only be a matter for conjecture. It certainly makes for a good story.

Dracula scholars have argued, convincingly, that Bram Stoker was inspired as much by Countess Bathory as by Vlad the Impaler in his creation of the world's best-known vampire.

When Anthony Cheetham - then editor at Sphere Books - asked me to write this novelisation of *Countess Dracula*, I had already been closely involved with the Countess for several years.

I first came across a mention of her in Ornella Volta's stimulating book, *The Vampire*. It immediately struck me that Elizabeth would be a perfect subject for a gothic horror movie.

At the end of the sixties,*The Countess Bathed in Blood* was one of two treatments I submitted to American International Pictures, producer/distributor of Roger Corman's Edgar Allan Poe movies. AIP optioned both treatments and I joined the company's London office as junior story editor (*house hippy* might be a more accurate description).

Selling the idea was, of course, only the beginning. Legendary exploitation producer Harry Alan Towers dashed off a screenplay, closely based on my treatment, with the title *Blood Bath*. Unfortunately - or perhaps fortunately - AIP suddenly fell out with HAT over *Sumuru*, a film he had produced (and Jesus Franco directed) for them in Brazil. This gave me the opportunity to write my own script.

Over the next year I was asked to rewrite the script for a variety of bizarre reasons. First, a part had to be written for AIP's major contract star, Vincent Price. Then all references to nudity and sex and wrinkly necks had to be removed in order to appeal to the ageing Joan Crawford, at that time making schlocky horrors like *Berserk* and *Trog*. (Barbara Steele remained my own first choice to play Elizabeth.)

When AIP ran short of ideas for new Poe films, Elizabeth's name was hastily changed to Berenice and the project retitled Edgar Allan Poe's *The Blood of Berenice!*

In 1969 AIP entered into a promising partnership with Hammer Films to make *The Vampire Lovers*, based on LeFanu's *Carmilla*, a character possibly inspired by Elizabeth Bathory. Ingrid Pitt - fresh from a strong role in *Where Eagles Dare* - was chosen to play the lesbian vampire. The Bathory project, with its similar mix of blood-letting and eroticism, would have been the obvious follow-up. Unfortunately, although *The Vampire Lovers* turned out to be one of Hammer's more stylish films, the executive styles of AIP and Hammer proved incompatible and no more direct co-productions were attempted.

Within a year I had left AIP to go freelance and was working part-time for Sphere Books as a horror and film consultant. When Anthony Cheetham asked me if I would like to write a novel for them, I suggested the Countess Bathory story. Anthony was enthusiastic and I began research in earnest. The next time I saw him, however, he had some surprising news. Sphere had just acquired novelisation rights to three new Hammer horrors about to go into production and one of them, *Countess Dracula*, was based - by pure coincidence - on the Bathory story!

As a film, *Countess Dracula* has much in its favour. It's beautifully lit, atmospheric, and Ingrid Pitt gives it her all - which is considerable. She almost succeeds in banishing nightdreams of *la grande Barbara*, Martine Beswick or Soledad Miranda in the role. And, of course, it's always a real treat to see the late Nigel Green (who plays Dobi) in anything. What is disappointing is that the film is so *restrained*. It comes across more like a BBC costume drama than a full-blooded Hammer horror movie. Remember those 600 slaughtered virgins? The body count here is about *four.*

It was left to Harry Kumel *(Daughters of Darkness)* and Walerian Borowczyk *(Immoral Tales)* to explore more fully the potential for erotic and surreal excess that the Bathory legend offers.

I am grateful to Nigel Wingrove, Pete Tombs and Redemption for giving new and sumptuous life to *Countess Dracula,* and for allowing me the opportunity to correct the plague of printers' errors which crept into the original edition. Along with a few infelicities of my own.

My long association with Elizabeth Bathory continues.

My original screenplay - newly revised as *Blood Beauty* - is of interest to producers wishing to take advantage of low costs and authentic locations behind the punctured Iron Curtain.

At the same time, I have embarked on a novel which resurrects the Countess and brings her to present-day London in search of fresh blood.

Enjoy this as an *hors d'oeuvre...*

Michel Parry

Lieutenant Imre Toth urged his horse to greater speed as he galloped along the winding forest path. He was late and the temptation came to dig his spurs into the animal's flank. He did not, as he knew he never would. Instead, he shouted encouragement in a firm, friendly voice that was loud over the beat of the gallop and the scattering of pine cones under hooves. The horse responded to its youthful master's shout and strained under the reins. Around them the hungry creatures of the forest rustled at the unfamiliar sounds, blinked their unseen eyes and slunk back into the darkest shadows.

It was a beautiful summer's day and, as he rode, Imre felt his face warmed by the sun filtering through the clawing pines. The light flashed golden on the gilt and brocade spangling his green leather tunic. He cut an attractive figure in his officer's uniform and black kepi, as many women had already noticed. Unfortunately, their speculations as to what lay beneath the uniform remained conjecture. Imre had preferred to retain his favours for someone special, rather than give himself to the painted kisses of soldiers' whores and camp drudges. As yet, the someone special had not appeared and, at the age of twenty, Imre was becoming more than slightly anxious to taste the pleasures of love. Older, experienced officers poked fun at him as they rattled their tankards above overflowing tables or fondled their drunken tarts. And Imre laughed with them, accepting their jokes with good grace, because he hoped, knew, that sooner or later...

Abruptly the crowding trees fell away and horse and rider emerged from the forest. So spectacular was the landscape now before him that, late as he was, Imre slowed his horse to a gentle trot to admire the view. Far below stretched miles of untamed forest, wild and thick as a gypsy girl's hair. Beyond rose the stern, black peaks of the Carpathians, the ruggedest mountain range in Eastern Europe. In the far distance the sun shimmered on their snow-capped heights. Imre found himself almost breathless, thrilled by the immensity of the spectacle. Such beauty, such purity, made his emotions soar. He swallowed a deep breath of crisp, mountain air, savouring it as he had seen others do as they sucked on their gnarled pipes. It felt fresh, invigorating. His whole body grew relaxed. A feeling of great contentment seemed to settle on him. Surely among such beauty, one could find peace. Not just an uneasy truce between kings or politicians - but true peace that one could feel inside oneself.

He noticed that a white curling mist was forming in the valley below. Already the openings to the mountain gorges were obscured. It was as if nature wished to hide herself from his prying eyes. The sight reminded him of the many legends told of this region, one for each rock, the old men said. All manner of creatures were believed to prowl the woods when the moon was full and high...vampires, ghouls, werewolves...and other creatures too terrible to have names. Imre thought how every inch of land must be drenched in blood - the blood of his countrymen and of many savage invaders - Huns Magyars, Bulgars, and, worst of all, the Turks.

Imre's boyish face was betrayed by a look of immense weariness, a look that was older than his twenty years should have allowed. His throat grew tight as he recalled the battlefield on which he had recently stood. He could see the frenzied faces of the demon Turks as they waved their curved swords; their hysterical cry - 'Allah, Akbar!', as they charged, again and again, beneath the crescent moon pennant. They fought like madmen, without care for their lives, since their heathen prophet had promised them the joys of paradise if they died in battle.

Swords hacked them, cannonballs pulped them and musketshot mowed them with Death's scythe. Yet still they came, goblin hordes shrieking blasphemy. Only death itself could check their lunatic advance. They laughed at gaping wounds and scurried forward on bleeding, crushed stumps...

There was one huge spahi who had come charging straight at Imre, lance poised to run him through. Five arrows had pierced the Turk, yet still he came on, face locked in a mad grin which showed all his teeth. Imre's legs had frozen and, helpless, he had stared at the sharp point of the lance as it rushed towards him. Then, suddenly, someone had pushed him aside and stepped forward to strike the Turk's head from his body with a single stroke of an axe. Undaunted by this discomfort, the headless body had run on a few yards before finally collapsing and spraying Imre with an arc of warm red blood.

The images came faster now: the blackened faces, bestial with fear or bloodlust. The sparks leaping from clashing swords. The ear-shattering blast of the cannons. The ghastly objects lying in slippery red mud. The wailing wounded. The panting screams of horses. The puking stink of spent powder. And worst of all...the stench of blood, the sweet sickly smell of human blood...

Beneath him, his horse shuddered as if it sensed his disgust. Imre extended a reassuring hand and patted its neck. At his touch the animal grew calm again. Imre looked behind him into the dark forest. It was not good to linger when Turks and brigands were never very far away. With affectionate noises, he urged his horse on and started up the mountain trail.

Presently, the horse rounded a bend on the tortuous path and Imre had his first sight of his destination. Castle Veres was a stark black pile squatting among blacker rocks. It looked so primitive that it was difficult to believe it could have been built by human hands, any more than the surrounding rocks were. Some way below the castle stood a poor village, where Imre could see smoke from cooking fires and signs of activity. Bordering the village were the pleasing greens of a wood. Probably full of deer and other game, he thought. And he could see the silver thread of a waterfall cascading down the rocks. The sight brought a satisfied smile to Imre's lips. Amidst such beauty he was sure to enjoy his stay at Castle Veres. It seemed just what he needed to relax and to forget the recent horrors of war.

Yet, curiously, it was death that had drawn him there.

Count Ferdinand Nadasdy was wearing his favourite uniform, the blue one with the baggy white trousers. It was his favourite because he had worn it at the battle of Mohacs many years ago. He had been explaining a tactical manoeuvre to the King of Hungary when a Turkish arrow had struck the King in the throat. He had died in the Count's arms, smearing his jacket with blood. The Count had not had it washed since, as he was fond of telling people. He was not telling anyone at the moment because he was dead.

In death the white haired Count looked better than he had done in the last twenty years of life. He was probably happier too as his old friend Fabio had observed. He had observed it to himself because it was dangerous to make some observations aloud. Critical remarks were somehow always conveyed back to the ears of Ferdinand's wife, the Countess Elizabeth. And now that his friend and benefactor was dead, Master Fabio was being very careful to remain on good terms with the widow.

To the black-coated undertaker inspecting him, the Count was just another piece of cold meat. Admittedly a richer, more exclusive type of cold meat than the usual. The sly-eyed undertaker stared down at the Count in his coffin, admiring his handiwork. The white locks were combed neatly into place and the food had been brushed out of his drooping moustache. Of the musket wound that shattered the old man's chest and ended his life, there was no visible sign.

The undertaker smiled wryly. There was no pity in him for the old Count. He had no particular reason to like or dislike him, any better than the rest of the nobility. They were all cruel tyrants, who would have you slit in half if you so much as looked at two kröners' worth of their property.

The undertaker was more ambitious than that. Making sure his fool apprentice wasn't spying in, he reached out and plucked the two gold coins that covered the Count's eyes and dropped them into his purse. Satisfied, he looked down at this silent victim. The Count's unblinking brown eyes stared accusingly. The undertaker took pleasure in a short contemptuous laugh. Then he dragged the heavy coffin lid over the Count's resting place and slammed it noisily into position. The Count disappeared from sight, stare included.

The undertaker sighed and smoothed his greasy hair. He called out for his apprentice. The boy ran in, a tall gawky youth whose gaping mouth declared his feeble wits. He was not exactly the most brilliant pupil, but then, if he were intelligent, his parents would never have sold him so cheaply. The undertaker patted the coffin lid affectionately.

'Nail it down and be quick. We don't want his lordship going off for a stroll before the funeral.' He sniggered to himself.

Anxious to please, the boy hurried to the coffin, a hammer in one hand, thick heavy nails in the other. He began to fumble one of the nails into position. The undertaker watched his clumsy efforts and grimaced impatiently.

'Hurry it up!' he barked. 'You don't want to keep the

Countess waiting. Not unless you can do without eyes in your face and a tongue in your head!'

Countess Elizabeth Bathory, widow to the late Count Ferdinand Nadasdy, was bored. Her little foot tapped out her displeasure beneath her long black dress. Would the service never end! Her hard grey eyes glared out at the other mourners from under her veil. Poor fools! They looked so ridiculous in their black clothes, like bedraggled crows. A movement among the grim black figures made her look up. At last! Something was happening. Stiffly, solemnly, four of Captain Balogh's bailiffs bore the Count's coffin to the side of the newly dug grave and laid it down carefully. As the bailiffs retreated, the priest began to intone more Latin verses which no-one could understand. Oh no! The Countess stifled a groan. At this rate they would all starve to death and join Ferdinand before the day was over.

Some distance away stood a cluster of peasants, mostly dressed in dung coloured rags. They stared at the group of black-clad mourners with intent expressions. A few were awed. A couple of shovelfuls of earth in an unmarked grave was all they could expect. Others were openly contemptuous, enjoying the suffering of their tormentors. Among these was Maryska, a dark haired woman whose worn features made her look about forty five. She was twenty five, but hard work and early child-bearing had left their impression on her frail body. Before her stood her two scrawny sons, Georgy and Sergei, one aged eight, the other ten. She nodded towards the funeral party and spat.

'Good riddance,' she said approvingly. 'That's one less bastard to work the poor.'

Her husband, Grigory, the cow-man, turned to her. He was a stocky powerful man, but his voice was gentle.

'Quiet, woman,' he said. ''Tis wicked to speak ill of the dead. And he wasn't a bad sort. Not like that wife of his... He promised me work. God rest his soul!'

Maryska scowled.

'Aye, there'll be work all right. For the worms! They don't care if a man be master or serf.'

Around her, several tattered villagers chorused their agreement. Shaking his head, Grigory took the hand of his younger son,

Sergei, in his own calloused grip and moved away.

'Come, woman,' he said without looking round.

Maryska stared at the stark figure of the Countess for another moment, then with a satisfied smile she turned and followed her man, the other boy trudging behind her.

Beside the grave the priest was still intoning the service. The Countess's angry eyes bore into him, willing him to finish. But he was unaware of anything except the potency of his words. The Countess turned away sharply, searching for fellow sufferers in her discomfort. Opposite her, Captain Balogh, the Chief Bailiff, stood starchily, arms behind his back. A suitably pious expression fidgeted on his face. The Countess snorted quietly. He was probably sincere as well, pompous ass!

On her own side of the grave stood Fabio. The old fool was nodding to the priest's words, eyes wet behind those ridiculous little round glasses he wore. He, of course, could probably understand the damned foreign gibberish.

The Countess shifted her scrutiny to Captain Dobi next to her. He stood in his usual effortless military stance. On his face there was a heavy-lidded look of disciplined patience. He seemed to have the ability to shut the rest of the world out at will. The Countess vainly wished she had the same gift.

As the priest's words droned on, Countess Elizabeth's eyes sought interest further afield. Suddenly, something caught her attention. She stood entranced, her irritable mood melting away.

Riding towards them, through the cemetery, came a young soldier, resplendent in his close-fitting green uniform. The Countess's old eyes gleamed. He was beautiful. She had not seen so handsome a man for years. Or perhaps she had simply not noticed. As he rode nearer, the sun behind him, the Countess was reminded of the enchanted Prince in the fairy stories that Julie, the nanny, used to tell her daughter Ilona. He sported a fine soldier's moustache, but there was more of the boy in his face than of the man.

She watched him dismount and hand the reins of his chestnut mare to a servant to tether. Then he strode towards the funeral party, his curved sword swinging at his side. The Countess tore her eyes away from the handsome stranger and looked enquiringly at Dobi. Catching the movement he turned and followed her gaze.

'General Toth's son,' he said, his deep voice lowered to a whisper. 'It was the Count's wish to have him here for the will.'

Imre Toth removed his fur kepi and held it under his arm as he walked towards the mourners. He was embarrassed at being so late. Nervously, he swept his loose brown hair back. He headed for the only person he recognised, Captain Balogh.

As the young lieutenant took up a position beside him, Balogh's beefy face looked up and formed a silent rebuke. Imre apologised with the look of a guilty schoolboy and lowered his head respectfully in the direction of the grave. He could not understand the priest's words but he had heard them often enough after a battle to know the service was coming to an end.

Without looking up, Imre became aware that somebody was staring at him. The feeling was very strong and oppressive. He lifted his eyes and looked.

At the other side of the grave stood an old woman, small and shrunken-looking. She was completely enveloped in a heavy black coat and a black hat partly hid her face. The rest of her face was heavily veiled, yet Imre could feel the power of her eyes as she stared at him. Of course, he realised, this must be the widow, Countess Elizabeth. He imagined the grief-stricken face beneath the veil and the vision came to him of his own mother as she lay on her death-bed.

The Countess continued to look in his direction. Perhaps she was offended by his lateness, worried Imre. Apologies would have to be made. He lowered his head towards her in the suggestion of a bow. Imre could not see her reaction beneath the veil, yet he had the impression she was smiling at him. Not a timid, weepy-eyed widow's smile, but a full-blooded suggestive smile. He felt discomfort and averted his eyes.

There were only three other people on the same side of the grave as the Countess, Imre remarked. This set them aside as being of special distinction. They must be noble friends of the late Count, he decided, or perhaps administrators in the rule of Castle Veres. To the right of the Countess stood a tall commanding man in his early fifties. He was dressed in barbaric black furs as befitted a warrior. There was an aloofness about him as though he was not part of the congregation but a disinterested observer. He was powerfully built, with huge arms and hands that looked like they could crush a man with the ease of a bear. Not a man to choose as an enemy, decided Imre.

On the Countess's left stooped a wizened old man with a long grey beard. He wore peculiar little spectacles, behind which Imre saw the sparkle of tears. The greybeard had the appearance of a man of learning and his clothes reminded Imre of a woodcut he had seen depicting the heretic, Erasmus.

Beside the old man stood a woman almost as old. Her nose was big and her features long and horselike. Such ugliness gave her an almost mannish aspect, yet it did not disguise an evident motherly quality. Her bearing reminded Imre of a nun or a nurse. As he watched her, her expression remained the same fixed mask. A benign, almost smug expression.

Imre suddenly became aware that the priest had finished speaking. He returned his attention to the ceremony. The priest eased the prayer book shut and stepped aside as four of Captain Balogh's bailiffs approached the coffin. Working quickly, the bailiffs ran ropes underneath the black box. Then they took up positions at each corner of the coffin. Heaving on the ropes, they lifted the coffin clear of the ground and manoeuvred it into place above the yawning grave. With almost painful care they began to lower the coffin into the earth.

The mourners craned forward, watching the Count's body being laid in his final resting place. Everyone's gaze was fixed on the coffin. Except for one person. The Countess. Her eyes were riveted on the handsome young soldier.

Grigory, the cowman, and his family had almost reached the village. Without speaking, Grigory left the muddy coach road and walked across a field towards an emaciated-looking cow. Behind him trudged Maryska and their two young sons. Maryska looked pityingly at her husband as he approached the raw-boned animal.

What good is a cowman with only one cow, thought Grigory. And such a cow. He glanced at the dull eyes, the withered udders, ran his hand over ribs that protruded like sickly growths. He shook his head despairingly. Soon he would not have even this wretched creature.

'Grigory!'

Grigory looked up sharply, responding to the alarm in Maryska's voice. Picking his way through the mud with dainty steps was Krantz, the money-lender. Grigory's spirits sank lower. He had no wish to see the money-lender that day.

'Good morning,' exclaimed Krantz, as he accosted Grigory, a smile on his face like a man sitting down to a good hot meal. 'I trust you've not forgotten what day it is?'

Grigory shook his head wearily. No, he hadn't forgotten about the three hundred kröner Krantz had loaned him.

'And you have the money?' asked the money-lender eagerly.

Grigory had used the money to buy four cows. They had been good milk-givers and he would have made a fine profit on them, if the pestilence had not come and killed three and left the fourth a diseased shell.

'No. I haven't got the money,' replied Grigory wearily.

'What!'

The money-lender's temper reared like an angry weasel. He gripped his gold-topped cane with rage.

'You refuse to pay!'

Frightened, the two boys clung to their mother's skirts. Maryska appealed to Krantz:

'Don't you see? We can't pay.' She nodded towards the ailing cow. 'This is all we have left.'

Krantz's eyes flicked disinterestedly over the beast. Their problems were no concern of his. He turned to Grigory, peering coldly into the larger man's face.

'Surely you remember the terms of our agreement? If you fail to pay, I get all your goods...' He thrust the cane forward with emphasis...'And your home.'

His face set, he turned and started back towards the road.

'Wait!' cried Grigory anxiously.

The money-lender paused and flung back, 'You have until this evening!' Then he strode away and for a moment there was silence except for the jingling of coins in his purse.

Grigory faced his family with a heavy expression. He saw the boys looking up at him expectantly. Their legs were no thicker than twigs. They hardly seemed in better condition than the cow. He knew they would never survive the chilly nights if they were thrown out of their home. Desperately, he looked towards the village. He had to do something. Anything.

The funeral procession was making its way slowly back to the castle from the cemetery. The grim colourless parade seemed unreal, nightmarish, as it passed by summer meadows with their flocks peacefully grazing in the morning sun.

The Countess was in her black open carriage, drawn by four horses of the same colour. Immediately behind the coach rode Captain Balogh and, at his side, Imre. From his position, Imre could see the tiny figure of the Countess sitting sternly upright opposite the fur-clad warrior. He noticed that she never once turned to right or left to view the passing countryside.

Silent villagers lined the route, anxious to catch a glimpse of the Countess in her moment of supposed grief. As she passed they doffed their hats, or touched a grimy hand to their foreheads. This display was born out of fear rather than respect. They knew that discourtesy was swiftly punished.

If the peasants hoped for some recognition of their efforts, they were disappointed. To the Countess they did not exist. She rode the jolting carriage with a disdainful expression, her flinty eyes staring straight ahead. They bore through Captain Dobi as if his seat were empty.

Captain Balogh cursed and gestured impatiently for two over-curious urchins to get out of his way. The children scuttled aside and Imre smiled at their terror. Then his attention was drawn to a man in the crowd ahead. The man was a hefty fellow, though obviously in need of food. What made him stand out among his fellows was his lack of servility. Ignoring the humble expressions of those around him, he glared defiantly at the Countess's oncoming carriage. Imre saw the man turn and mutter something to his neighbour - a dark-haired, hollow-cheeked woman clutching two scrawny boys. Then the man stepped into the road and up to the carriage.

'Countess...your husband promised me work!'

The Countess heard the man's words but did not look round. The impudent beggar, she thought. He would pay dearly for this insult - when there were less eyes to see his pain.

Getting no reaction to his plea, Grigory walked alongside the carriage, easily keeping up its pace. The Countess was sitting there as if she had not heard him. Perhaps she was hard of hearing, he thought. Somehow, he must get through to her, make her understand about his children, his home. Desperately he reached out, gripped the door with his big callused hands, trying to attract the Countess's attention. The coach seemed to be going faster now and he had to half run to keep up. The Countess's face remained averted.

As the man clutched the door of the carriage, Dobi eyed him coldly. He admired the man's pluck, but his action could not, of course, be tolerated. Otherwise every runny-nosed serf would be demanding special treatment.

'Be off!... Away with you!' commanded Dobi in a deep resonant voice accustomed to giving orders. The man hung on, staring beseechingly at the Countess in a way that almost made Dobi laugh out loud. Seeing no movement to comply with his instruction, Dobi casually raised his riding crop and brought it down hard on the man's hand. The man winced, but retained his precarious hold on the carriage. Wild-eyed, he addressed the Countess, his voice quivering with emotion.

'Countess, I beg you...my wife and boys are starving!...'

Again Dobi's riding crop slashed down on his fingers. They were quite bloody now, but he refused to let go, his forgotten dignity returning in a burst of defiance for the arrogant masters that fate had inflicted on him.

'In the name of God!...He promised...He gave his word...'

The Countess wrinkled her nose. The creature's vile-smelling rags were definitely an insult to well-bred nostrils. She caught sight of the driver, turning to her for instructions. She gave a curt nod and instantly the driver whipped up the team. The horses protested with shrill annoyance. Then the carriage lurched forward, gathering speed.

The cow-man yelled as he feet were swept from under him. Vaguely, he was conscious of screams as he clung on desperately to the jolting door. The steward was slashing again and again at his hands. He could feel the blood flowing warmly down his arms. But the carriage was racing along now and he knew that if he let go, his head would splatter like a rotten melon. He gritted his teeth. The ground was flashing by, tearing at his legs, flailing the skin from them...

Imre watched helplessly as the peasant was dragged along by the speeding carriage. It seemed impossible that the man could be taking such punishment. Then the carriage jerked as the wheel hit a rock. His hold broken, the man was lifted like a puppet into the air. He slid back and, screaming, disappeared beneath the carriage. There was a dreadful shriek and a snap like wood breaking. An instant later, he emerged from under the back wheels and rolled to a stop, limbs spread awkwardly.

Imre reined to a halt beside the man and was about to dismount when he saw that the carriage was continuing down the road with extraordinary violence. He realised the driver must have lost control. His look of alarm was reflected on Captain Balogh's face and, together, they urged their horses in pursuit.

Shrieking her grief, Maryska ran up to the body. Behind her came her two sons, sobbing and confused.

A glance was enough to confirm her despair. The wheels had crushed Grigory's chest and the splintered ribs had punctured his lungs. His eyes stared unseeingly at the sky and a bloody froth issued from his lips. Maryska threw her arms in the air and wailed her loss. Other peasants gathered round and, seeing the body, crossed themselves vigorously. Maryska brushed the wetness from her face with her sleeve. Then, howling curses, she began to run after the escaping carriage.

Rocking and jolting, the Countess's carriage plunged into the village of Veres. Frightened villagers leapt for their lives as the panting horses thundered by.

Galloping full out, Imre was slowly catching up with the runaway vehicle and Balogh was not far behind. Imre could see the Countess sitting rigidly in the reeling carriage. She did not seem at all concerned and Imre saw her companion's teeth flash as he threw his head back and laughed.

The carriage and its pursuers sped through the narrow streets of sloping whitewashed houses. The team cleared the village and careered up the approach road to the castle. It loomed up blackly. The portcullis was down and it seemed certain that the carriage would crash into the gates, dashing its occupants against the wall.

With seconds to spare the driver expertly reined in the team. Their fury spent, the horses slowed to a halt and placidly waited for the gates to be opened.

Feeling foolish, Imre and Balogh pulled up behind the carriage. Dobi's sardonic smile was waiting for them and Imre flushed, angry with himself for his rash display.

As the gates were lifted, the sound of running made Imre turn. Some way behind, a woman was stumbling towards them. Imre recognised her as the woman the dead peasant had spoken to. Her hair was in disarray and her face twisted by grief and hatred.

Suddenly, she stopped, jerking as if someone had punched her in the stomach. She swayed unsteadily, then recovered her footing and shook her fist angrily in their direction. Her words, spat out like curses, carried clear and loud.

'Devil woman...Devil...Devil!'

Imre glanced towards the carriage. Beneath her veil, the old Countess seemed composed. There was no indication she had even heard the woman's abuse. Again the Countess nodded and the carriage moved forward. It rumbled through the castle gates and out of sight. Captain Balogh started to follow after it.

Imre looked back towards the woman. She sank to her knees and the sound of her sobbing reached him with dreadful clarity. Imre hesitated, wanting to help the wretched woman.

Captain Balogh looked impatiently back at him. 'What are you waiting for?' he demanded. Then he saw the young soldier was still staring at the cow-man's widow. His flabby jowls quaked as he laughed.

'Don't waste your sympathy on a peasant, there's too many of them!' Chuckling to himself, he spurred his horse in the wake of the carriage. Uncertain, Imre glanced back once more at the weeping woman. Then, slowly, he followed Captain Balogh.

The great metal doors of Castle Veres clanged shut, loudly and resolutely, on Maryska's grief.

Imre was waiting in the castle library as Balogh had instructed him. It was a large library, one of the biggest Imre had ever seen, and crowded with shelf after shelf of ancient leather-bound volumes. The air was oppressively musty and Imre found it necessary to pace about in order to avoid being overcome.

Casually, he started to inspect the books, which were arranged in categories. Mathematics...Etiquette...The Scriptures. Nothing to interest him there, he thought. Astrology...Occultism...Witchcraft...He smiled. Perhaps those strange and horrible stories he had heard about the Count's ancestors were true after all.

This was more like it! A whole section on warfare, battles, strategy. Things a young soldier could understand. He reached out and took down a copy of 'Caesar's Conquest of Gaul'. Flicking through the yellowing pages, he thought of the hours he had been made to study it at the Military Academy. Shaking his head, he replaced it and moved on.

Here was a copy of his father's own book on tactics. He took it down and opened it. On the fly-leaf was an inscription. The words were faded and he deciphered them with difficulty: 'To my dear friend Ferdinand who taught me much that I know.' It was signed in his father's hand.

The sound of approaching feet made him turn and he started in surprise. The Countess was seated by a big old desk. How could she have come in without him hearing, he puzzled. She was still wearing her veil, but she appeared to be staring intently at him. He nodded and smiled at her, wondering if she was still angry at his lateness. He had seen something of her temper earlier, although she was not really to blame. The man had brought his death upon himself.

Imre was relieved when Balogh swept into the room. Following him were the Countess's three companions from the funeral. The others sat beside the Countess, while Balogh busied himself behind the desk. He shuffled impatiently through a disorder of papers, before fishing out a large scroll with a heavy seal. The Count's will.

Satisfied, Balogh looked up and smiled paternally when he saw Imre. He cleared his throat to attract the attention of the others.

They looked up expectantly.

'Before we proceed with business,' he began, 'I'd like to take this opportunity to present Imre Toth...'

He gestured in the direction of Imre, who put the book down and stepped politely forward. The others turned to look at him, with the exception of the rugged-looking warrior, who lounged further back in his chair.

Balogh leaned over towards the Countess and whispered by way of explanation, 'The son of your husband's late friend General Toth.' Then he drew himself to his full height, which included a feathered hat, and addressed Imre.

'The Countess Elizabeth Nadasdy,' he announced.

With a flick of her wrist, the Countess threw back her veil. Imre hoped his face did not betray what he felt on seeing her face. He had been told that the Countess was in her fifties. The woman before him seemed more like she was in her sixties or seventies. Her face was entirely creased and pitted by a network of wrinkles. He realised he had seen exactly this effect on ripening corpses after a battle. Still, her powerful grey eyes looked kindly on him and her smile was sweet.

'Enchante, Countess.'

Imre bowed from the waist. The Countess extended her heavily jewelled hand. Imre took it in his own. It was light as a glove and unnaturally cold. He pressed his lips to the hand, warming it with his breath.

As he straightened, she gently squeezed his hand. She nodded, the same provocative smile lighting up her withered face. Again, he thought that some hot and lustful spirit must be trapped inside this dying shell. The grasp lingered and Imre recalled his earlier discomfort at the cemetery.

Balogh was saying, 'Captain Dobi, the Steward of the castle.'

Imre looked up from the Countess's hypnotic eyes and towards the proud-looking warrior. Dobi honoured him with a brief, haughty glance, then dismissed him.

The old greybeard seemed more anxious to make his acquaintance.

'Master Fabio, the historian and archivist.'

So the old man was a scholar. Fabio nodded enthusiastically at Imre, a broad smile struggling through his whiskers.

That left the horse-faced woman.

'And Julie, the Countess's...' Balogh hesitated, groping for the right word. 'The Countess's companion,' he decided.

Julie fixed Imre with a bland smile as he offered her a curt bow. It was the same expression she wore at the funeral. He had yet to see it change.

The introductions completed, Imre made his way back to the Countess and seated himself in a vacant chair on her left. Balogh spoke to him again:

'One person not yet arrived is Ilona, the Countess's daughter. Her father sent for her when he knew he was dying,' Balogh explained. 'Alas, too late.'

The Countess sighed and flourished her hand imperiously. 'Yes, yes...get on with it,' she commanded as if the reading of the will was a tiresome formality, whose contents had already been revealed and digested.

The feather on Balogh's hat quivered with resentment. Although the Countess was his superior by birth, he was responsible to a higher authority than her and expected better treatment. Emotions bristling, he lowered his eyes and busied himself breaking the seal. He remained standing, as this seemed to make the proceedings more official. The breaking of the seal was performed with some ceremony and took so long that the Countess twice shifted position amid many rustlings of her black robe.

At last the scroll was unfurled and the group sat up with eager apprehension. Except for Imre, who confined his attention to inspecting his nails. He felt slightly ridiculous being present on this occasion. Obviously the others expected substantial bequests. What could he look forward to? At best a tattered standard. Or maybe a rusting sword, the obligatory tribute from the Count to a dead friend's heir.

'The last will and testament of Count Ferdinand Nadasdy,' read Balogh.

'It's quite brief,' he observed, daring a rebellious look at the Countess. She glared back and he quickly returned to the will. 'To Captain Dobi I bequest my arms and uniforms...' Balogh looked up at Dobi, surprised. Dobi was surprised too. He sat up, disbelief subverting his usually stern features. He stared at the document as if its existence was a personal insult. Then, he uttered a short bark of contemptuous laughter and fell back in his chair with forced amusement.

The Countess watched this exhibition with enjoyment. When she was satisfied that she had derived maximum pleasure from the situation, she turned to Balogh and gravely nodded for him to proceed.

'To Julie Szentes...' Balogh looked up, hoping to catch some new expression on the nanny's bland visage. He was disappointed...'one thousand kröner and food and lodging in my home for the rest of her days,' continued Balogh. Still her fixed smile did not change.

Beside her, Master Fabio shuffled uneasily and tugged on his beard. He knew it was his turn next.

'To Master Fabio my library and all contained therein,' was Balogh's pronouncement. Delight illuminated the scholar's face. He clapped his hands and slapped his knees. He shouted 'Ho ho!' repeatedly and would have gone on doing so, had he not caught Balogh's tolerant glare. Coughing apologetically, he restrained his pleasure to a broad smile.

'To Imre Toth...' Balogh paused and all eyes turned towards the young outsider. Despite himself, Imre looked up at Balogh, keen excitement stirring.

Balogh resumed his reading. 'Son of my dearest friend and army companion, who fought gallantly with me and saved my life on more than one occasion...' Balogh glanced briefly at Imre, then continued. 'I bequeath my famous stable with all the horses and the cottage.'

For a moment no one seemed to believe what they had heard. Dobi's firm jaw quivered with rage beneath the grey stubble of his beard. His black eyes blazed towards Imre. With an exasperated cry, he threw himself from his seat and strode angrily across the room. At the door he hesitated and, seeing the Countess's reproachful look, he composed himself and slumped against the wall. He resumed glaring at Imre.

Imre had not spoken. He hardly dared believe his good fortune. Was he really master of one of the finest stables in Europe? A few days ago he would have laughed at the suggestion and now it was fact! Balogh's voice cut into his thoughts.

'We now come to the most important part of the will.' His voice took on a reverential tone. The others were silent, glancing at the Countess.

'To my beloved wife, Elizabeth,' read Balogh, 'I leave my fortunes and estates...' Balogh paused significantly, looking to the Countess for her reaction. She was smiling, her expectations fulfilled. Concealing his enjoyment, Balogh continued: 'to be equally divided with our only child, Ilona.'

The Countess's smile vanished. She sat bolt upright, her face hard, eyes fierce and incredulous. Imre could scarcely recognise her as the same sweet-smiling old lady whose hand he had kissed. Dobi evidently shared her disbelief. He looked towards the Countess, expecting an outburst.

With some effort, the Countess controlled her seething emotions. Nodding to Balogh, she slowly said: 'We must respect his wishes.'

'That concludes this main business,' announced Balogh. 'Now for the servants' bequests. Would you ask them to come in, Captain Dobi?'

Dobi stepped to the door and, opening it, signalled for the waiting servants to enter. As they filed in and nervously grouped around the desk, the Countess rose from her seat and turned to Imre. He jumped to his feet and took the opportunity to address her.

'Madam, I must apologise for my late arrival. My horse lost a shoe.'

She was looking up at him, expressionless. Her eyes probed his face. He waited for her rebuke. Then her thin lips jerked into a smile.

'Well, now you have all the horse shoes...and the horses that you need.'

He smiled back at her, relieved to hear her responding with good humour.

'And as you are to be my new neighbour,' she continued, 'we shall doubtless see much of you. At least I hope so...'

Again Imre sensed that lurking suggestiveness, the youthful desire trapped in her ageing flesh. He found himself replying with undue formality. 'The honour will be mine, Countess.'

She held her smile for a moment longer, then stepped past him out of the room. Julie and Dobi made after her. As she passed, Julie offered Imre her benign countenance. Dobi pointedly ignored him and swept past. Imre watched him go, hoping he had not made an enemy on his first day.

Feeling a tug at his sleeve, he turned to find Fabio's friendly face blinking up at him. The scholar nodded knowingly towards the bookshelves.

'I noticed you were reading something when I came in,' he said confidentially, as if reading were an activity to be spoken about in whispers. Perhaps it is, inside this gloomy castle, thought Imre. He gave a short laugh.

'That was just something about soldiering I picked up,' he replied, thinking it wise not to mention that his father was the author. He did not want this merry sage to think him a numbskull.

'No matter, it's rare enough to come across a soldier that can read,' chortled Fabio. 'Still,' he continued, 'I daresay you're more interested in horses than in dusty old books and manuscripts.'

'I'm afraid you're right, Master Fabio,' admitted Imre, thinking it fortunate he had inherited the stables and not the library.

'You wish to see these famous stables?' inquired Fabio.

'Indeed I would!' said Imre, warming even more to the old man.

'Then come with me.' The old man was already making towards the door, with the stiff-legged gait of the aged.

Imre looked back at Balogh. He was still addressing the servants, his voice droning, ' to Josef, my faithful servant, two cows of his own choosing and any offspring thereof.' Imre quickly followed after Fabio.

He caught up with him in the corridor. He was aware that the Countess had stopped at the other end of the corridor and was huddled in discussion with Dobi and the mannish nanny. He did not look round. Instead, he tried to be as friendly as possible to Fabio as they proceeded along the corridor. It would be good to have an ally in the castle if Dobi were to prove disagreeable in the future.

'It seems you've inherited a fine library, Master Fabio,' he offered.

'The finest in the land,' replied Fabio, with a contented flourish. 'You cannot imagine my delight.' He chuckled to himself, thinking of the rare prizes contained in the library.

As they continued, Imre noted that the walls of the corridors were tapestried with scenes from the bloodstained history of Veres Castle and the Nadasdy family. Battles...conquests...murders...all lovingly recreated and immortalised at the artist's loom. Imre shuddered to think of the sights that the grim silent walls must have witnessed. He was not aware that, behind him, the Countess had turned and was watching him with a hawk-like intensity.

They rounded a corner and emerged into a gallery overlooking the huge and austere main hall, with its shadowy timbers. Imre's attention was attracted elsewhere. Coming towards him was a rosy-cheeked chambermaid of about sixteen. In one hand she carefully carried a lightly-smoking copper pan. Fabio was holding onto Imre's arm with a friendly grasp. 'I feel that you too are something of a scholar, my friend,' he suggested hopefully. Imre did not answer. He was too busy studying the wench as she swayed nearer. She had perfect unblemished skin and huge innocent eyes. Imre felt sure that her skin would feel like satin if her reached out and touched her.

As she passed, their eyes met. Conscious of his admiration, she smiled provocatively and blushed. For a brief moment she hesitated, entranced by the handsome young soldier. Then she skipped by.

Imre turned to watch her go and was pleased to see that she too was looking back. He smiled at her, broadly and invitingly. She giggled and hurried on. Imre became aware that Fabio had noted his interest in the girl and was watching him with amusement. His mind groped for an excuse.

'What was she carrying?' he asked, striving for a note of genuine curiosity in his voice.

They had started descending the massive staircase leading down into the main hall. Fabio turned to him.

'A pan of coals,' he guffawed, 'the solace of widows and lonely fools.' He cackled mischievously at his own wit. Then seeing that Imre was still puzzled, he drew closer and whispered confidentially, 'It makes her cold bed hot.' Imre's hearty laughter joined in with the old man's.

Teri, the chambermaid, advanced dreamily down the passageway, ignoring the handle that was becoming too hot for her hand. She was thinking of the brave-looking soldier, with his kind eyes and white teeth. He had seemed to like her, enough to turn round and get another look, anyway. Maybe he would come to her little room one night. Or make a secret meeting in the rose garden by the light of the moon. Perhaps he would be the one to rid her of her wretched maidenhead...She bit her lip to stop a giggle.

'Teri!' The harsh voice cut cruelly into her reverie. The old hag of a Countess was standing before her, glaring angrily. The Countess caught hold of her arm with long, bony fingers. Teri winced as she felt sharp finger nails sinking into her soft flesh. The Countess's terrible eyes transfixed the frightened girl. She was so close that Teri was almost stifled by the awful smell of her decayed breath.

'You're paid to work, not dream, girl,' said the Countess, showing her teeth as she spoke. 'Now, get on with it.'

She pushed Teri's arm away as if it were a disgusting object.

'Yes, Ma'am,' whispered Teri. She made a rapid curtsey and hurried away. She gripped the heating pan as tightly as she could, even though it was scorching her palm.

The Countess lifted her trailing black skirts and walked quickly to the balcony overlooking the main hall. She moved at a pace rather faster than was thought respectable for a widow. At the balcony she paused, taking pains not to be seen from below. Fabio and the young soldier were walking through the hall towards the door leading to the stables. They were both laughing and the old man was repeating something aloud as if the sound of it pleased him. She strained to hear and the words drifted up faintly.

'Keeps her cold bed hot!'

The words hit her like lash. Her thin lips became thinner. Without Ferdinand, there was no one to champion the old fool. He had better be more careful in his choice of jokes, she thought. If not...Elaborating on the possibilities, she swept back to her bedchamber.

Unaware of the compliment the Countess was paying him, Master Fabio opened the heavy wooden door leading out to the stables. Imre was staring glumly at the huge sombre portraits of past unsmiling Nadasdys. Above them hung tattered standards and pennants, unstirred by the wind for centuries. Fabio saw the look on his young companion's face and chuckled comfortingly. 'There are worse places to live,' he said. 'And when Ilona returns...'

The words trailed off with a hint of blissful promise. Imre's spirits rose at the thought of someone his own age, his own class and, especially, of the opposite sex.

'Has she been away long?' he asked.

'Since she was six years old,' the scholar replied. 'They sent her to Vienna to escape the dreaded Turks.' His voice grew warmer. 'I'm told the gods have favoured her. She's a great beauty, the idol of the court. As her mother once was.' His eyes glazed with remembrance of things past and his look became nostalgic.

'Though you'd never think it to see her now,' he added wistfully.

Shaking his head at the cruelty of time, he put his arm round Imre's shoulder. Together they stepped out into the fading daylight.

In the Countess's bedchamber, memories hung as heavily as the musky perfumes that permeated the rich hangings and drapes. The red velours, green satins and exotic silks were themselves part of her memories. They had accompanied her to the castle as part of her dowry and had hung in this room ever since. The Countess clung to her memories like a starving man to bread. To her they were as vivid and brilliant as the tiny flames dancing above the green and purple candles that dimly lit the room. For years she had retreated into her recollections of her youth, preferring them to the loneliness of reality.

It had been Ferdinand's fault, she told herself. Always off to some distant war, leaving his young bride to cope with a baby and an estate. No wonder she had aged and withered before her allotted time. Eventually, she left the care of the baby to Julie and the estate to Dobi and locked herself in her room. There, she began to put on one dress after another - she still possessed every one she had worn since her teens - reliving the memories they brought back...The finery and gaiety of the Viennese court...The music! She saw herself, a pale virgin, smiling shyly behind a fluttering fan, surrounded by admirers all eager for the next dance. They had been real gentlemen, the noblest in Europe, not boorish upstarts like Balogh. She cast his fat repugnant face from her mind and thought back to the delicate features of the late King. How divinely he had danced. They had been as light as clouds as they pirouetted together before the eyes of the court. She might have married him instead of Ferdinand if a Turkish arrow had not taken him out of her life.

How could she ever have married Ferdinand, she asked herself. Then when she remembered him as a young officer, she knew the answer. He had looked so dashing in his uniform, riding out to battle at the head of his men. She could still see his brown eyes looking sulkily out from behind long lashes. See him stroking his smoothly clipped moustache. (How like him that young Imre

Toth was, she realised.) Later, when they were married, he had allowed it to grow long and straggly, so that it trailed in his soup and his kisses tasted of forgotten meals, and she stopped kissing him. And now he was dead and buried, only another memory to be trotted out and contemplated in the long winter evenings.

The Countess's jaw set hard with resolution. She was not going to just fade away, another memory trailing in Ferdinand's wake. She was going to make up for those precious, lost years. From now on, she would embrace life passionately, as enthusiastically as a nun discovering sex. And if life refused to embrace her, she would find ways of forcing it to!

The Countess was sitting before her dressing mirror removing her jewellery. Her eyes shone lustrously as she gazed at the spreading heap of stones. There was a history behind every one of them and she could tell them all.

Behind her, Captain Dobi had settled his lean, sturdy body into an armchair, stretching his long legs out by the blazing fire. He was staring into the leaping flames and caverns of glowing embers, pausing now and again to take a swig from a cup of coarse red wine. Beside him on the floor stood an almost empty bottle of the fiery liquid. He gulped back the contents of the cup and reached down for the bottle...His system had long ago accustomed itself to large quantities of alcohol. On this occasion, it permitted him to feel slightly drunk and he was grateful.

At the back of the room, Julie fussed around, making preparations for the Countess to retire to bed. With loving hands, she turned down the bedclothes and laid out the Countess's nightdress, ready for use. Convention demanded that widows wore night-clothes of rough, chafing linen. The discomfort was supposed to remind them of their loss and make them offer up prayers for the dearly departed. The Countess's night-gown was of the softest, skin-caressing, blue silk.

Julie did not have to do such work,. It was really up to Teri and the other chambermaids. Yet Julie was not happy unless her hands were busy in the care of a loved one. She cared nothing for her own needs or appearance. She was entirely self-effacing. As long as she could please others there was meaning to her life, her shadowy existence was fulfilled.

Little Ilona had been the centre of her universe. When they sent the child to the safety of Vienna, her world had crumbled. She became purposeless, a pitiful creature like a spurned dog. Then she attached herself to the Countess, and Elizabeth, grateful for any kind of companionship, tolerated her and began to accept her as something more than a servant.

So encouraged, Julie came to worship the Countess as a mother worships her child. The bond grew until there was nothing Julie would not do for her. There was no scheme too cruel for her to participate in if it was blessed by the Countess's interest. For Julie, the Countess was always right.

Clutching his empty glass, Dobi began to laugh quietly to himself. The laughter grew into a rich melodic outburst. He became inclined to share his thoughts, repeating them aloud with sarcastic emphasis.

'Twenty years! Twenty years as Steward of this castle...protector of his lady...and what do I get for it?' He rounded on the Countess to give her the full benefit of his observation.

'A couple of suits of armour and a trunk full of old uniforms!' Again his laughter echoed round the bedchamber.

The Countess was examining her face in the dressing mirror. The network of wrinkles spread across her parchment skin like a contagion. The very sight of it made her sick to her stomach. Was there nothing that could stop the corruption and give her back her beauty? Every poultice, potion and half-baked spell she had ever tried had proved useless. Maybe it was a punishment , a judgement for her adultery. Ferdinand had robbed her of half her inheritance and God had taken her beauty.

Off hand, without turning round, she threw back at Dobi: 'What else did you expect?' She snorted. 'You think he was a fool?'

Dobi was looking at her, smiling. He did not see her wrinkles, her ugliness or her cruelty. He saw only the woman he had loved for years, while she was another man's wife. 'You're right! Who am I to complain?' he agreed, rising unsteadily to his feet. 'When in truth, he's left me the greatest prize of all!'

His right hand grasped for her. Impatiently, she got up, scraping her chair, and slipped past him. Safely out of his reach, she turned to confront him.

'I was not aware that I was bequeathed to you,' she said coldly.

'But don't you see, you're free now?' responded Dobi, certain there was nothing more to argue about.

'Yes, free to choose whom I please,' replied the Countess and hurried into the adjoining bathroom before he could say anything else.

The low, white marble bath was already nearly full to the brim with steaming water. Elizabeth moved to one of the shelves that were laden with ointments, lotions, unguents and pomades of every kind. None of them had proved efficacious in restoring her beauty, but she was loath to throw them out.

From one of the shelves she selected a sprinkler of sweet-smelling oil of Araby. She began to shake it energetically into her bathwater. Teri entered struggling with a large jug of boiling water. Her pretty face was flushed from the heat. With difficulty, she slopped the contents into the bath, precipitating a blast of angry white steam. The Countess stepped back, eyeing the water critically.

'Do you wish me to burn myself?' she snapped irritably at the girl. 'Fetch cold water quickly.'

Dismayed, Teri made a token curtsey and hurried out, clutching the jug.

Dobi pushed his way past the escaping chambermaid and entered the bathroom. Playfully, he advanced on the Countess.

'Have I got a rival?' he asked. 'Our new neighbour, perhaps?' The Countess smiled faintly at the ingratiating tone in his voice. He saw her smile and roared his amusement.

'That young puppy!' he shouted, laughing at the thought of the ageing Countess pressing her advances on the young soldier.

He reached out and pulled her urgently into his powerful arms. She seemed smaller and more delicate than ever next to his muscular body. It pleased him.

'Countess, I've loved you for twenty years,' he declared. She looked up at him, surprised at the unexpected sincerity in his voice.

'I've waited patiently for this day and now you're really mine,' he said proudly. He leaned down to press his lips to hers. She wriggled determinedly out of his grasp and stood back. She was touched by his affection and when she spoke, her voice was gentle. 'Please go. I wish to take my bath.' She moved back towards her beauty lotions.

Uncertain, he hesitated...It would not be the first time he had seen her naked body. Or the last. Why was she being so modest now, he wondered.

Sensing his hesitation, she turned and spoke more sharply. 'Leave me,' she ordered.

From her expression, he deduced the game was over. She was no longer acting the friend and lover, but the stern Countess. Dobi shrugged casually. He gave her a small smile to let her see his hurt, then, obeying, he awkwardly left the room.

Regretting her temper, she watched him leave. She turned back to the shelf and replaced the oil of Araby.

Behind her Teri entered with the cold water. She poured it steadily into the bath and dared a glance at her mistress. 'It's cooler now, Madam,' she announced timidly. Turning, the Countess peered speculatively into the water. Without warning, she grabbed hold of Teri's right arm and plunged it deep into the water. The terrified girl screamed in pain and struggled to withdraw her arm. With uncanny strength, the Countess held it down in the scalding water. Teri's face screwed up with agony. She whimpered, on the verge of tears.

'Cooler?' asked the Countess shrilly in her ear.

At last she let go. With a cry of relief, Teri jerked her arm from the water and held it to her mouth. The pain was throbbing and the reddened arm felt hot against her lips. She knew better than to stand about feeling sorry for herself in the Countess's presence. Painfully, she lifted the jug and poured the remainder of the cold water.

The Countess watched without speaking. She began to unbutton her black dress. Her mouth felt dry from the heat and excitement. She remembered the bowl of fruit on her table.

'Peel me a peach!' she commanded, without glancing at the chambermaid.

Teri hurried to the bowl of fruit and chose the ripest, reddest peach. From a drawer she took a small sharp knife. Her hands were trembling and she had difficulty in holding the peach because of the pain. She dared a look at her mistress. The cruel hag was removing her underclothes. Teri caught a glimpse of drooping, wrinkled breasts, hanging pendulously.

The knife slid into the peach. The sticky juice ran out and felt cool on her burnt hand. She began to rotate the peach, slicing off the skin and revealing the firm yellow flesh. Her hands were running with juice now. Suddenly, the peach slipped right out of her hand and fell soggily to the floor.

The noise spun the Countess round. She saw the peach on the floor and advanced angrily towards the frightened girl.

'What are you trying to do? Turn the room into a pigsty?'

Teri started to protest that her hands were burnt, but then the Countess was striking out, slapping at her face with long-clawed hands. Instinctively the girl raised her hands to protect her face, forgetting she still held the knife. The Countess lashed out again - jerking Teri's hand - and the knife slid into her cheek as easily as through the peach. She screamed as she saw blood spurt redly onto her hands and felt the hurt. She threw the knife down and clasped her hand to the spilling wound.

The Countess was still now, though glaring furiously at her. Across one side of her face was a red smear where the blood had sprayed her. She looked disgusted.

Teri burst into tears and, covering her face with her hands, she fled from the room. She ran past a startled Dobi and out into the corridor and up the servants' stairs. She did not stop running until she reached the safety of her own lightless room. Then she threw herself onto her bed and the bed shook as a spasm of sobbing convulsed her body.

The Countess had a way of upsetting her servants, so Dobi took little notice of Teri's emotional exit. Instead he filled his glass to the brim again and watched Julie tidy up the Countess's jewel box. He watched her smug face as she plucked the gems off the dressing table and wondered if she had ever been tempted to steal any. Probably not, he decided. The only things Julie found beautiful were fat, gurgling babies.

'Julie!...Dobi!' There was something harsh and unnatural about the Countess's voice. Something that made them instantly alert, running for the door to the bathroom. What they saw as they entered made them pull up short. The Countess was sitting in a darkened corner of the room, gazing at her reflection in the dressing mirror. To her face she clutched a blood-stained cloth. Dobi's first reaction was to think the Countess had cut herself. Yet there was no pain in her expression. Instead there was something he had never seen in her before - an ugly mixture of exhilaration and awe. Dobi recognised the look. He had seen something like it before on soldiers' faces. It was the look they got when they ran amok through the streets of captured towns, killing and maiming defenceless men, women and children. It was the grim mask of blood-lust.

Still holding the cloth to her face, the Countess looked up at them.

'It's the blood,' she whispered. 'The girl's blood!'

Her wild eyes strained to see into the darkness behind them.

'Isn't she here? Where is she?' Her darting eyes fell on Dobi.

'Bring her to me.' It was more of a plea than a command.

Dobi's lip curled with disgust. So she had tortured her chambermaid and wanted more of it. He felt sickened. Torturing a prisoner of war for information, he could understand. But not some poor child of a serving girl. Where was the profit?

'What do you want with her?' he asked.

The Countess's eyes appealed to him.

'Please...bring her to me.'

He softened under her gaze. He would have done almost anything for her in response to such a look. But not this. Not harm an innocent child. 'No...Find yourself some other amusement. Excuse me.' He bowed curtly and strode from the room.

The Countess remained seated. She rested her gaze on Julie who had not moved. There was concern behind the benign smile as Julie watched her mistress. She had never seen her looking so strange. It must be the stress of the funeral, she decided.

'Julie...please.' The voice did not sound so pathetic now. The Countess was regaining her forcefulness. Julie still hesitated, not knowing what to say.

The Countess saw that Julie's attention was fixed on her. Very slowly, she took the cloth from her face and let it drop. Julie's gasp of shock and amazement was loud in the silence of the room. The Countess turned back to her mirror and inspected her face. The side which had been smeared with blood was now as smooth and unblemished as a young girl's - in hideous contrast to the wrinkles and lines disfiguring the rest of her face.

For years she had been searching for the secret which would give her back her youthful beauty. And now she had found the elusive solution. And it was far cheaper than oil of Araby or any of her other expensive, useless concoctions. In fact, it was the cheapest commodity on the estate - the blood of a peasant.

The Countess turned back to Julie who was still looking at her in disbelief.

'Julie...please fetch her.'

The nanny remained too astonished to reply. Hesitantly, she moved forward to inspect the Countess's skin more closely, a look of delight and approval creeping across her bland features.

The Countess addressed her sharply.

'Very well, if you won't, I'll fetch her myself.' She stood up, her face registering determination.

'Take me to her!' Julie knew it was an order that could not be disobeyed. Casting another quick look at the miracle that God, in His wisdom, had bestowed on her mistress, Julie hastened out of the room. The Countess followed.

In her dark little room, Teri had stopped crying. Her eyes were red from her tears and her face was streaked with blackly-drying blood. She lay on her bed thinking she must escape from the Countess's domain, away from her taunts and jabs. Perhaps that nice-looking soldier would help her. She wondered how far she would get before the bailiffs caught up with her. Or perhaps she would be captured by Turks and forced into a harem for one of their fat officers. Even that would be preferable to this miserable existence. She looked towards the tiny barred window. It was just like being a prisoner.

Startled, she sat bolt upright as the door creaked open and the Countess entered. Behind her Julie's thin figure appeared.

Tensely, Teri waited for an outburst of anger. None came. Instead the Countess gave her a reassuring smile and came and sat on the bed next to her.

Teri could hardly believe it. The old bitch seemed genuinely sorry. Reaching across the bed, the Countess took the girl's face in her hands and began to gently caress her cheeks. At the same time she began to softly hum a lullaby, one she had often sung to Ilona years ago.

It was very soothing. Teri began to relax. She felt forgiven and forgiving. The thought of running away now made her feel guilty. After all, the whole thing had been her fault. She managed to smile sweetly at the Countess, trying to show her gratitude.

Without stopping the lullaby, Elizabeth grasped the cut on Teri's face between thumb and forefinger, and twisted viciously. Teri shrieked and the blood began to flow again.

Beside the door, Julie watched without a change of expression. After a moment, she carefully shut the door, locking the sound of the girl's torment into the small room.

Dobi was striding through the village streets, trying to block out the smell of refuse and unwashed bodies. He was in a bad mood as he made for the main entrance to the castle. He had paid a visit to the Shepherd's Inn, but all the girls had been taken, so he had returned with his mission and his desires unfulfilled.

He passed a group of singing children without a glance. The urchins were dancing in a circle chanting -

> Ring a ring of roses
> A pocket full of posies
> Atishoo, atishoo
> All fall down!

At the climax, they all fell to the ground as they had seen the plague victims do. A moment later, unlike the plague victims, they all leapt back to their feet, laughing and shouting.

As he strode through the main doors, Dobi saw a procession of servants crossing the main hall. They were grouped around Rosa, the red-faced cook. Her fat features were creased with anxiety and there was a note of distress in her voice as she appealed to the other servants.

'She went up to the Countess's room last night and that's the last I saw of her...Her bed isn't slept in...'

She broke off as she noticed Dobi approaching them. Dobi had hardly noticed her, his attention being fixed on a couple of very pretty kitchen maids. He was wondering if they were partial to a small bribe.

Rosa waddled up and thrust her fat face at his. 'Oh, Captain,' she whined, ' have you seen my daughter? Teri, the Countess's chambermaid? She's disappeared and I'm so worried.'

Dobi was in no mood for hysterical mothers. He pushed irritably past her.

'How should I know where she is?' he snapped. 'Try the whore-house,' he added and started up the stairs.

Rosa's sagging features drooped further and her expansive breast began to quake with grief.

'She'd never do that,' she bawled. 'She's a pure girl.'

She took out an onion-smelling handkerchief and dabbed at her red eyes.

Ilonka, one of the less attractive kitchen maids, put a comforting arm around Rosa and glanced up at Dobi's receding back.

'He'd know if she was in the whore-house,' she commented knowingly. The others murmured agreement. Then, offering gloomy advice about the wild ways of young girls, she led Rosa away by the arm. The whole party retreated towards the kitchen.

Dobi was making his way down the main corridor towards his bedroom. As he passed the Countess's bedchamber, he heard a happy cry from within: 'Dobi!...Julie!'

It was unlike the Countess to sound so happy these days. He walked back to the door and listened. There was no sound within. He knocked on the door and entered. What he saw inside made him cry out and slump to his knees in supernatural terror.

Standing before him was the Countess - but the Countess as she had been thirty-five years ago.Gone were the wrinkles, her skin was soft and smooth and deliciously white. Her cheekbones were high and her lips full and sensuous - made for love. She laughed at his astonishment, eyes sparkling with the vitality of youth.

He fumbled questions as his eyes prowled hungrily over her body. Her breasts were ripe and firm, bursting out of a low cut, blue silk night-dress that rode to the tops of her thighs. Smiling invitingly, she moved towards him on perfect legs. He could see her nipples straining darkly against the night-dress.

Overwhelmed by her beauty, Dobi rose shakily to his feet. He stretched his arms out pleadingly.

'What have you done?' he cried and made a sudden lunge towards her. He wanted to press her against him to make sure he was not dreaming.

For an answer, she flicked her honey-blonde hair at him and danced lightly away. Laughing, he tried again. She evaded his clumsy caress.

Breathless, he leaned against a wall, suddenly feeling how old he was in contrast. An idea came to him and he looked around wildly. What if this were a trick? Not the Countess at all, but an impostor. She laughed again and he thought of springtime, many years before. When he looked back at her, he knew it really was the Countess standing before him.

'Where is she?' he appealed.

'Who?' asked the youthful Countess teasingly, still enjoying his confusion.

He gestured helplessly round the room.

'The girl...the chambermaid!'

'No one will find her,' she said finally.

Dobi stared long at her, stunned by her beauty, appalled at how she came by it. It took all his willpower for him to tear his eyes away. The change was incredible, terrifying. There was nothing he could say.

'Look at me, Dobi.'

The voice was sweet but insistent. He looked, warily. She curtsied like a shy debutante and her laughter rang out. He stared at the creamy valley between her breasts and knew he would do anything to lie there.

'I'm ready for my first ball,' she teased and sprang lightly up again.

Dobi shook his head as it to clear it. He found his voice at last and the words came in a steady assault. 'And what will your daughter say?' he demanded. 'She'll be here tomorrow. She'll find her mother the same age as she is!'

She looked hard at him and the knowledge he saw behind her eyes was that of the old Countess.

'Will she be here tomorrow, Dobi? she asked him in a teasing voice.

Questioningly, he looked at her as she moved to him. Her warmth yielded against his body. Her hands pressed against his chest and began to work down. Her lips brushed softly against his cheek. He shook gently as he felt her tongue burn moistly into his ear.

'Will she?' repeated the young Countess.

Ilona Nadasdy surveyed the passing countryside from the window of the heaving coach. She was looking for the familiar sights of the land she had left twelve years previously. So far she had seen little other than trees, and trees looked pretty much the same everywhere.

The sight of silver butterflies dancing among the tree-tops brought a happy smile to her lips. She was pleased to be back and looking forward to seeing her parents again, after such a long separation. Her pretty blue eyes grew moist and troubled again. She did so hope her father's health would be improved when she arrived! Perhaps he might already have recovered and would be waiting to greet her by the huge wooden door when her coach pulled in. And her mother too. She wondered if her mother was still as beautiful as she remembered.

Ilona herself had grown into a beautiful girl, the toast of the Viennese court. Her blue eyes were kind and open and beneath her pert little nose pouted a pair of adorable pale lips...Brown hair fell in attractive ringlets to below the collar of her long, green velvet dress. The puffed sleeves were white and transparent, permitting a glimpse of exquisitely shaped arms lightly covered with golden down.

Without warning, the coach came to a bumping halt, horses neighing disapprovingly. Alarmed, Ilona poked her head out of the window to see what was happening. The driver, a greying man of surly temperament, was strolling down to the river, bucket in hand. Lifting her voice with urgency, Ilona cried out to him.

'Please hurry! My father may be dying! I must get to the castle before nightfall...'

Ignoring her, the driver plunged his bucket into the cool, running water and hauled it up for a drink. Ilona sank impatiently back onto the faded red plush of her seat.

After a few minutes delay, the driver reappeared, whistling casually. He climbed back into the driver's seat, whipped up the team and the coach pulled noisily away. Neither Ilona nor the driver were aware of three pairs of hostile eyes watching them from the cover of the forest.

In the coach, Ilona relaxed and sighed with relief now that the journey was resumed. She felt as if she had been thoroughly shaken - like a dice in a cup - all the way from Vienna. The road was better now and she began to forget her discomfort, knowing that in less than an hour, she would be embracing her mother and father. They would expect a young lady schooled in Vienna to have attained a certain standard of gentility in dress and behaviour. Vigorously, she began to brush her long brown hair.

Two loud shots made her drop the brush clattering to the floor and cry out in fear. Glancing out of the window, she saw two fierce-looking brigands with smoking pistols riding down to intercept the coach. One of them wore a red bandana round his head like a gypsy. Beneath it a wily brown face leered at her. The other had greasy hair brushed back and fearsome black brows. Aiming his pistol, he called on the driver to halt.

Above her, the driver whipped the team to greater speed with urgent cries. Cursing, the black-browed highwayman fired again. Ilona screamed as the driver clawed his blood-spurting face and fell into the road.

Seeing the coach driverless, the Szigany spurred his mount and soon caught up with the frightened leaders of the team. He grabbed the harness and forced them to a halt, cursing prolifically. Blackbrows dismounted and walked straight up to the coach. He threw open the door, and pulled Ilona struggling from the carriage. Seeing his wild-eyed look, Ilona feared more for her virginity than her life. She drew herself up and prepared to fight dearly. The brigand threw back his greasy head and laughed, showing big, ugly, stained teeth. Then, with effortless ease, he picked the girl up and flung her across his saddle. He jumped up after her and, holding firmly onto the kicking girl with one arm, he rode away, followed by the gypsy.

From his hiding place, Dobi had watched the whole scene. He waited until the two cut-throats had disappeared with their hostage. Then he urged his horse out from the cover of the bushes and set off for the castle, his mission accomplished.

Imre was having difficulty choosing himself a horse from the selection the stable-lads were steadying before him. He had never seen such excellent mounts, not even in the cavalry. He moved enthusiastically from horse to horse, inspecting an eye here, a foreleg there. It was a difficult choice but finally he decided. He pointed to a magnificent black stallion. Quickly, the stable lads hastened away the rejected horses, while the chosen stallion's handler began to saddle him for Imre.

A friendly greeting made Imre turn to see Fabio approaching, a large map rolled under his arm. The old scholar walked with small brisk steps, rolling from side to side in a way that made Imre smile. He hurried up, eyeing the stallion warily.

'Are you satisfied?' he asked.

'As you with your library,' returned Imre. He looked from the horse to Fabio. 'Come ride with me,' he suggested.

As if outraged at the suggestion, the horse reared up, protesting. Fabio scuttled back as the stable boy tugged the stallion's head down with a rope.

'No, no,' Fabio declined. 'The creatures terrify me!'

He unfurled the map and help it out to Imre.

'But I brought you a map of the area for fear of losing you already.'

'Thank you.' Imre took the map and inspected it, impressed with the old man's gift.

'And the Countess would deem it a pleasure if you would dine with us tonight.'

Something in Imre's face must have betrayed his reluctance to accept, because Fabio continued, 'Don't look so miserable.'

In truth, Imre was not looking forward to renewing his acquaintance with the Countess. There was something about the Countess that repulsed him. She reminded him of an old toothless whore, painting herself up to look young. The Countess would not go so far, but Imre sense the same hunger for youth.

'The fair Ilona arrived at dawn,' revealed Fabio with a meaningful wink.

'And is she as beautiful as you said?' demanded Imre.

Fabio shrugged. 'I haven't seen her yet. She's been closeted with her mother all day.'

Imre calmed his frisky black mount and confidently swung into the saddle. Fabio tensed, expecting to see the boy fly off the black devil's back, but Imre sat comfortably. The horse was acting as gentle as a puppy.

Imre looked down at the greybeard.

'You've convinced me of the need to attend,' he said, laughing. ' I shall see you there.'

Swinging the horse round, he began to make for the main gate.

'We dine at seven!' added Fabio, shouting from cupped hands.

Across the courtyard, Imre reared the horse and waved in acknowledgement. Fabio watched him ride away, wishing he had been a father.

Ilona's upside down journey thorough the forest, helpless in the hands of the brigands, was quite the most terrifying thing she had ever experienced. She thought she was going to faint until she realised that she was much too interested in what was happening to lose consciousness.

However, the blood rushed to her head as she dangled precariously over the saddle and the jolting of such an inauspicious means of transport made her stomach lurch. She was very relieved, if still anxious, as they reined up outside a wretched-looking woodcutter's hut. Her eyes and mouth were full of dust and she was only vaguely aware that someone had emerged from the hut and was approaching them.

'Here's your delivery, Janco,' announced Blackbrows. Her captor jumped from the horse and roughly pulled her down after him. Landing awkwardly, she cried out in pain. Her head was reeling after her ordeal. Dazed, she raised herself and examined the man at whose feet she had landed. The first thing she noticed about Janco was an enormous slimy black moustache, drooping from beneath a hooked nose and slanted, Mongolian eyes. The second thing was that his clothes were indescribably filthy. His rough sheepskin coat was matted with dirt and a no less repulsive fur cap squatted on his bald head.

As she looked up, he performed an angry little dance and admonished the bandits for their bad manners with a series of guttural clicks and grunts which made no sense to her at all.

Turning his peculiar attentions to Ilona, he extended towards her a hand richly coated with dirt. Not being in a position to complain, she took hold of it and he helped her to her feet with surprising gentleness. Taking a couple of steps back in his huge fur boots, he clicked his heels and made an extravagant bow in her direction.

The two bandits laughed uproariously. The sight of the bedraggled would-be courtier was so funny that Ilona almost laughed as well, despite her situation. Janco straightened up and smiled toothlessly at her, if such a hideous expression could be called a smile.

Still laughing, the bandits spurred their horses and sped quickly away. Clicking excitedly, Janco grabbed hold of Ilona's hand and began to pull her towards the hut. God help me, thought Ilona, I've been delivered into the custody of a madman!

Before her huge dressing mirror, Countess Elizabeth was inspecting her new body, as she had been doing all morning. She feasted her eyes on the golden hair, the delicate complexion, the soft curves...Even now, she could hardly believe the change herself. Every time she looked in the mirror, she was pulled up short, half-expecting to see the familiar haggard face, the lifeless grey hair...Hopefully, they were no longer a part of her life.

Julie was helping her into an evening dress, a beautiful red velvet gown the Countess had commissioned for Ilona. Now it seemed more fitting that she herself should wear it to dinner.

'How do I look?' appealed the Countess for the fiftieth time that afternoon. 'Do you think our new neighbour will find me irresistible?'

'Is there anyone who can resist you?' responded Julie fondly.

Deftly, her fingers tightened the already clinging dress and the Countess's generous decollete was further exposed.

Eyes sparkling, the Countess laughed delightedly. It was true. No one could resist her. She hugged Julie, bathing her in the warm glow of her happiness. Everything was perfect, and tonight she would possess the delicious young soldier. Unless he were no man at all, or his loins were made of stone.

As Imre entered the main hall, still flushed from the excitement of his ride, he was greeted by Master Fabio, wringing his hands in glee.

'We are in luck,' he gloated, putting his arm round Imre. 'The Countess is overcome by the reunion with her daughter and will take dinner in her room.'

Imre's spirits rose. The only cloud on his horizon was lifted.

'And the daughter?' he inquired, trying to sound disinterested.

Fabio clapped his hands.

'She will be down!'

They sensed someone approaching and, turning, saw Dobi swaggering towards them. There was an awkward pause. Imre felt Dobi's stern eyes watching him from beneath their bushy brows. He hoped Dobi could be appeased, before hostility set for good.

'You two have met before, I believe,' said Fabio, stepping in skilfully to bridge the gap. Imre was going to politely answer, when he saw that the words had not even penetrated to Dobi. The Captain was staring helplessly upwards. Imre followed his gaze and felt the breath drawn out of him as an ache swelled in his chest.

Standing at the top of the stairs was one of the most beautiful girls he had ever seen. Her beauty was almost too perfect.

Her hair, seemingly woven from pure gold, spilled down onto

creamy bare shoulders. Her perfect curves were caressed by a daringly cut gown of red velvet, that made little secret of her attractions. Imre judged her to be about twenty years old.

Regally she descended the staircase, followed by Julie. Even old Fabio seemed bewitched by her charms. He scuttled forward to greet her.

'My dear young lady,' he said, blinking excitedly through his glasses. 'Do you remember me?'

The young Countess smiled confidently back at him.

'Dear Master Fabio, how could I forget you?'

Graciously she held out her hand for him to kiss. Smirking with pleasure, Fabio dipped down and brushed it with his lips. As he did so, he peered up at her through his spectacles, seeing her smiling face closely for the first time. Fabio's brow creased in perplexity. The Countess noticed his surprise.

'Have I changed that much?' she asked, sounding concerned.

With scarcely a pause, Fabio tactfully extricated himself. 'As a flower changes from bud to bloom. Past recognition,' he gushed.

Under the watchful gaze of Julie and Dobi, the young Countess moved towards Imre, who waited breathlessly. If possible she looked more beautiful when seen close to.

'And this is my young friend, Imre Toth,' Fabio informed her with a gesture.

Her smile was warm and inviting. Imre took her hand and pressed his lips to the dainty fingers. He longed to kiss his way up her gold-flecked arm, across her gently heaving breast, up to the mysteries of her full lips. Realising he had held her hand longer than expected, he released it reluctantly.

They smiled at each other, their youth establishing an immediate bond in the grim, oppressive castle.

'My mother has spoken of you,' she said in a voice that was young and light, but had the sound of authority behind it.

'Your father and mine were, I believe, the closest of friends.'

Imre thought he could detect something more than polite friendliness in her voice. Could she be feeling the same attraction he felt for her? He dared hardly hope.

Imre nodded. 'As I hope we shall be,' he hazarded. Then, not wishing to be thought too forward, he added, 'Your mother, I hope she's not too unwell.'

'No, merely fatigued.'

There was a curious amusement in her eyes as she spoke.

'She asks us to dismiss her from our minds and enjoy ourselves this evening.'

So saying, she turned to Dobi and lowered her eyes at him in a satisfied manner, secretly delighted at the success of her playacting.

Dobi gravely stepped forward to meet her.

'Shall we eat?' he asked, taking her arm and leading her to the banqueting table.

Automatically, the young Countess stepped to the head of the table and prepared to sit.

'No, that's your mother's chair,' rebuked Dobi, staring at her dead-pan. There was the slightest hint of irony in his deep voice.

The young Countess hesitated, aware that they were all watching her. Damn Dobi!

'Of course,' she replied innocently. 'Tonight I am taking her place in more than one respect.' She sat down and the others followed her example.

In Janco's hut, Ilona was seated dejectedly at a small wooden table, waiting for her supper. In front of her, the strange creature was stirring a pot of food that bubbled over a smoking fire. She toyed with the wooden spoon Janco had laid before her. She had discovered that Janco was not a madman, at least not entirely. His muteness was due, not to derangement, but to disability. She shivered as she thought of the black space in his mouth, where other people had a tongue. It had probably been cut out by the Turks, or because he was a thief. The last was more likely the truth, she decided. It occurred to her that she was probably being held to ransom. Perhaps a note had already been delivered to the castle, demanding payment. She hoped the news would not upset her father as he lay on his sickbed.

Dejectedly, she looked around at her surroundings. It was a filthy hovel, full of the most ridiculous and useless objects. The remains of a cart filled one corner. Everywhere underfoot was dirt and old bones. Janco seemed to share the hut with two goats and assorted poultry. The smell was sickening.

She did not know that Janco had made some effort to enliven the surroundings for his guest. A single flower curled out of a mug in the centre of the table.

A series of jocular grunts announced that supper was ready. Janco approached and placed two plates of steaming food on the table. Her nose twitched suspiciously. Rice and fish, she decided, hunger disappearing. Janco spluttered noisily at her, exhorting her to eat.

Ignoring him, she stood and walked over to a bowl of oily water. She pursed her pretty lips grimly. It would have to do. She began to wash her hands.

Janco watched her ablutions with eyes wide as a cod's. He had never seen anyone waste water like this before. Glaring back at him, she wiped her hands on a piece of rag and returned to her chair.

The mute lurched forward and dipped his hands into the water. Splashing happily, he began to imitate her actions. Ilona sighed as she watched his antics.

After a couple of minutes, Janco tired of the new diversion and joined Ilona at the table, hands still dripping wet. He was about to plunge his hand into his food, when he looked up and saw the girl practising a new novelty. She gathered a tiny portion of rice on her spoon and raised it doubtfully to her lips.

Ilona spat out the food. She had never tasted anything so foul. Janco did not appear to notice her verdict on his culinary ability. He was still staring at the spoon clutched in her hand.

Excitedly, he looked around for another spoon. He failed to find one, which was not surprising because Dobi had only provided him with one. Ilona watched, horrified, yet fascinated, as he cupped his right hand in imitation of her spoon, scooped up a handful of the vile mess and raised it to his lips. He slobbered it down, grunting appreciatively.

Ilona couldn't stand it any more. He was making a fool of her! She flung her plate at his head, splattering him with glutinous rice. She leaped out of her chair, sending it crashing down, and ran for the door, scattering chickens and angry cats in her flight.

The door was locked. It withstood her strongest efforts, as she shook and pulled it.

Behind her, Janco clawed the soggy mess from his face and crammed it into his mouth, sucking his fingers clean with the air of a connoisseur. He watched her, his expression less friendly than before.

Beneath the warm glow of the blazing flambeaux, the figures at the banqueting table made merry. Their emotions had been mellowed by glass after glass of spiced wine, then inflamed by large portions of hot peppery paprika stew. Loud and joyous rose their voices, exploding at intervals into roars of indulgent laughter. Everyone was warm with drink and flushed with pleasure. Even Dobi and Imre were like re-united brothers, raising their glasses to one another in mutual admiration.

Dominating the company was the young Countess. She entertained them like an experienced hostess. Her conversation came fast and fluid, her wit sparkled and had them helpless with laughter. They guffawed into their dripping glasses and repeated her sayings aloud, until the hall echoed with merriment.

During a break in the laughter, Imre asked her: 'Can you remember anything of your life here?'

'Yes, indeed.' The wine that had loosened her tongue now tripped and slowed it, but the others hung onto her words with close attention.

'Many things...one story...in particular...the day of my departure...' She paused and glanced knowingly at Dobi. He met her look and, unnoticed by the others, his smile wavered. He clenched his glass more tightly. Without giving her a chance to continue, he rose to his feet, forcing warmth back into his expression. The others turned to hear him.

'I offer a toast to the new arrival!' He held up his glass and inspected the rich red liquid. 'With the wine so much loved by your dear father...' He nodded politely in the direction of the young Countess. 'Not just the taste, he used to say, but the colour...' Dobi paused to make sure he held everyone's attention...'of bull's blood.' The last word was drawn out significantly. Then he lifted his glass and drank.

Following his example, the others rose unsteadily, holding out their glasses to the young Countess and murmuring agreement. 'To the new arrival!' they cried, wishing her well for having lifted the veil of gloom from the castle. Then they drank, and, senses ablaze, dropped back into the plush chairs.

As he sat, Dobi again addressed the Countess and only she discerned the savage irony in his voice.

'Forgive me, Countess Ilona...please continue with your delightful story.'

The Countess laughed confusedly, and held a hand to her head.

'I cannot remember,' she apologised.

There were playful cries of disappointment, chiefly from Fabio.

'The day of your departure,' prompted Imre hopefully.

'Ah, yes - I was swimming in the lake, and -'

She lifted her head back and her joyful laughter rang out, as if she were witnessing the incident anew...

'There on the bank,' she resumed, 'I saw a man cutting blooms - who could it be? A gardener? Too upright of bearing. A thief? He was just too far away for me to recognise, and...' Her voice sank to an indulgent whisper...'Modesty forbade me from leaving the water!'

She paused as there were loud guffaws from around the table. The laughter died and the circle of faces waited intently.

'Later, I saw the same roses in my mother's bedroom,' she continued. 'I asked her who had given them to her. "One of my secret lovers", she replied.'

Again there were cries of pleasure from the listeners. Only Dobi remained aloof, watching her sternly.

'What did she mean? She promised to tell me when I grew up. And tonight, before I came down to dinner, I had my answer. And the name of the man?'

She looked around at the expectant faces. Her voice rose on a high note of triumph, as she flourished towards the end of the table.

'It was Uncle Dobi!'

She burst into delighted laughter, which the others took up and amplified. All except Dobi. Glaring down from the other end of the table, his face betrayed embarrassment and anger.

Ignoring him, the Countess stood up, indicating the end of the meal. Her companions stood as well as their legs permitted them.

'But I have spoken enough about myself...'

She extended a hand pointedly in the direction of Imre. Throwing down his serviette, Imre moved round the table and took her hand with enthusiasm.

'Help me to rediscover my home,' she appealed, '...and tell me about your life, your plans, your family...'

As she spoke, they headed towards the stairs. In passing, she darted a quick look of triumph at Dobi. Hand in hand, she and Imre started up the stairs.

Dobi sat down heavily. He was fuming, but powerless to act. At least for the moment. He realised Fabio was looking at him with interest. He outstared the old man and drained his glass. Then he banged it loudly back onto the table.

Together, Imre and the beautiful Countess roamed the midnight corridors. The wine had done its work well and they were both in excellent spirits, laughing uproariously and leaning against each other for support.

They paused beneath a portrait of an elderly, white-haired man. A whimsical smile graced his countenance, as if he successfully harboured a secret.

'My grandfather,' revealed the Countess. Her voice mockingly took on a haughty moral tone.

'His weakness was women. He died in the arms of a kitchen maid,' she added reproachfully. Imre smiled back at the old man. No wonder he looked contented.

'Then I salute him,' declared Imre and executed a very smart salute despite his condition. The Countess laughed spiritedly and clasped his arm. Imre felt wonderfully excited at having her so near to him. Every time he breathed, he was inhaling her seductive perfume.

They moved on to a portrait of a singularly ugly lady. 'His wife,' said the Countess simply.

Imre peered up at the condescending face. The subject's features were bloated and her eyes small and reproachful. It was easy to understand her husband's erring ways.

'No doubt a great beauty of her time,' said Imre generously.

Giggling, they proceeded up the corridor, hand in hand. The old Countess's bedchamber loomed ahead. The young Countess put a finger to her lips.

'Quietly past my mother's room.'

With exaggerated care, they tiptoed past the door, like eloping lovers. A portrait of Ferdinand Nadasdy looked benevolently down on them.

'Your father,' said Imre admiringly. 'What a brave and generous man he must have been.'

'Yes.'

Her voice lacked interest and he looked at her, surprised by such coldness. Perhaps it was understandable. She had not seen him for years and years, thought Imre.

'Does he look as you remember him?' he asked.

Her sparkling eyes skimmed over the Count's likeness. 'Much the same,' she said non-committally.

Suddenly they found themselves standing beneath a portrait of Countess Elizabeth - a portrait painted thirty years previously.

Imre was open-mouthed with astonishment. The similarity was incredible. Beside him stood the living embodiment of the Countess as the painting depicted her.

'My mother,' said the young Countess.

Imre nodded dumbly, lost in admiration.

'Do you find her beautiful?' she asked a little too casually.

Imre turned from the painting and looked directly at her. 'Irresistible!'

Pleased, she rewarded him with an enchanting smile and pushed him towards a door that was slightly ajar. She clasped her bare arms as if feeling the chill beginning to seep from the stone walls around them.

'I think I'll get my shawl,' she said and entered the room.

He followed her inside, unaware that Dobi was watching resentfully from the far end of the corridor.

The room was dark, lit only by the moon's brilliance and the light seeping from the corridor. Imre suddenly realised that Ilona was no longer in front of him. He looked around urgently. She was nowhere to be seen. His eyes were drawn to a large double bed with a scarlet coverlet. It looked very inviting.

Teasing laughter escaped from behind a nearby screen and Imre cried out accusingly. Entering into the spirit of the chase, he rushed behind the screen, but she evaded his grasp and, nymph-like, danced away across the room.

Emerging from behind the screen, Imre saw her standing by the window. The moonlight held her in its delicate embrace. It spun a filigree web of highlights around her golden hair, and fell glowing on her breast. Her paleness in the moonlight gave her a child-like quality. She looked quite irresistible. Quietly, Imre approached her with careful steps, as if afraid he would startle her into running away. He took her hands in his and pressed them warmly.

Without speaking, they stared into each other's eyes. He had not noticed before what depths her eyes had, or that they were grey, like her mother's. They seemed to hold limitless knowledge as if she were mature far beyond her years. It was a frightening thought and he cast it from him. He asked gently, 'Will you live here now, with your mother, or return to Vienna?'

Without averting her eyes, she said, 'I haven't decided. And you?'

He looked about enthusiastically.

'I already feel this is my home. The first proper home of my life.'

His face fell as an unwelcome thought occurred to him.

'But the war is not over yet and I may be recalled to duty.'

Subdued by this unhappy prospect, they both remained silent for a moment. When he spoke again, an optimistic note cheered his voice.

'But until that happens I shall stay.'

He held her fondly, feeling the warmth of love flow between them.

'And if you leave,' he promised, 'I swear to you, I shall take my horses...'

Her sweet laugh punctuated the solemn vow.

'All of them?' she asked teasingly, marvelling at the sincerity she felt in him.

'All of them' he agreed, 'and I feel I shall follow you wherever you go.'

The young Countess looked away from his ardent gaze and hung her head with mock humility.

'But I'm not worthy of such a sacrifice,' she protested.

Putting his arms firmly around her, he said, 'Let me be the judge.'

She did not push him away, as he had half-feared. He lowered his head and felt the heat of her breath trembling against his lips. Gently he nibbled on her lower lip. A small sound of pleasure escaped her. He pressed his own lips against her mouth, finding it moist and agreeable. She closed her eyes, losing herself in the intensity of his kiss. His passion mounting, Imre crushed her to him, his tongue probing her teeth for entrance to the warm pleasures of her mouth.

For a moment she yielded, then, drawing back, she broke away and danced frustratingly over to the door. Her feelings were mingled. She wanted to feel his love inside her, yet her better judgement told her that to be too hasty could be disastrous. He might lose all respect for her.

'No,' she said tantalisingly. 'We have our reputations to think of. After all we have only just met.'

Disappointed, Imre followed the young Countess to the door.

'When can I see you again?' he asked anxiously.

She seemed flustered, as though his question disturbed her, forced her to a difficult decision. Finally, she brightened, and, smoothing his cheek with her hand, said, 'On Sunday. We will ride together on Sunday.'

Inwardly he groaned. He could never wait that length of time. 'Two whole days,' he protested. 'Impossible.'

She smiled at his impetuousness, pleased that he was so eager for them to continue their relationship. It was impossible to refuse him.

'Tomorrow then,' she allowed. 'But late, when the others are asleep.'

She pondered a moment.

'Come to the small door below the tower. I will light a candle in the window above. That will mean all is well and you may enter.'

She turned anxiously towards the door, as if afraid that someone might be approaching.

'Now you must go,' she insisted.

Urgently, he took her in his arms again and found her lips with his own. The kiss did not last as long as before, but it was intense and eloquent. It revealed his love for her better than he could have put it into words.

Reluctantly, they parted their bodies. Her hand found his and held it tightly as he hesitated in the doorway. He blew her one last kiss and was gone.

The Countess moved slowly to the small window and peered up at the vivid moon. Her cheeks were flushed with excitement and apprehension. She bit her lip to stop it quivering.

Tomorrow, she foresaw, she would feast on his young body. And she would make love as she had not done in twenty years.

The pretty young peasant girls giggled and chased each other squealing as they returned from fruit picking. It had been a good day, and their baskets, carried in darkly stained hands, were piled with juicy berries, destined to be baked into pies for the Countess's table.

Julie hardly noticed them. She was too busy scattering seeds into the tall round cage that housed the carrier pigeons. The birds cooed appreciatively and fought, fluttering, over the choicest items. She marvelled how any creature could become so excited over so little.

Looking up, she saw Fabio approaching, his nose in a book as usual. Best place for it she decided. It kept him out of other people's business.

Fabio walked up and made clucking sounds at the pigeons. 'Tell me, Nanny,' he began conversationally, 'How do you find our little mistress? Has she not exceeded your wildest dreams?'

'In what way, Master Fabio?' she replied in her slow humourless fashion. Her starched white headpiece made her resemble a strict old mother superior.

'In every way,' bubbled Fabio. 'For a girl who is not yet nineteen, she is well...'

Groping for words, he flapped his arms restlessly, like one of the birds in the cage.

'So mature of bearing, so witty and confident in her manners...'

'Indeed,' interjected the Nanny without apparent interest. There was one fat old pigeon who always got the best pieces. She watched it calculatingly.

'But one thing puzzles me,' continued Fabio. 'I always thought she favoured her father.' He shook his head in bewilderment. 'And now I find she is the image of her mother.'

Julie impaled him with an icy glance. Her voice matched the smugness about her mouth.

'I think you grow old, Master Fabio. And your memory is confused.'

She turned and resumed her feeding of the pigeons. Their mellow cacophony recommenced.

Fabio sighed and shrugged. Everyone was treating him like an old fool these days - everyone except Imre.

'Let it pass,' he said wearily. 'One never argues with a Nanny.'

A mischievous grin spread across his face and, gleefully, he added, 'Not unless one wants a box on the ears!'

Laughing, he wandered away, pausing once to wave at Julie.

Coldly she watched him go. The fat old pigeon was still intimidating the others. Julie glared at him and began to savour the taste of pigeon pie.

It was night and the castle was a black smear against the starless sky. There was silence except for the prowling of night creatures. In the courtyard, Imre crossed the fragrant rose-garden and took up a position behind a sturdy chestnut tree. In its shadow, he knew he would be invisible to any casual observer.

In front of him rose the tower from which Ilona was to give her signal. As he anxiously watched, he could hear the leathery flap of bats circling the turret.

A figure suddenly appeared at one of the topmost windows. Imre waited with bated breath. A second later, his vigil was rewarded as a candle flickered into life at the window. Imre left his hiding place and moved down a path leading towards the tower.

As he reached the door, it swung open, revealing the young Countess. The candle she was carrying bathed her in a halo of light. Without speaking, she warmed him with her body. Then, cautioning him to silence with a finger to her lips, she led the way up the winding stairs, the candle throwing taunting shadows around them.

Fabio's eyes ached as he emerged from the library. He would have to stop reading so late, he mused, else he would lose his sight altogether. A sudden sound brought him up sharply. Further down the corridor, a marble fireplace was slowly swinging open...Clearly, the person using the secret entrance had no desire to be seen and Fabio ducked back into the library and soundlessly swung the door shut. A moment later, he had recovered his astonishment and felt brave enough to open the door a crack. As he peered into the half-light of the corridor he saw Ilona and Imre pass by arm in arm, looking cautiously about them.

When they had passed, he opened the door a little further and poked his head out into the corridor. The young couple were disappearing into Ilona's room. Fabio smiled into his beard, admiring the success of his young friend. Yet something disturbed him.

Imre was abusing the Countess's hospitality and her punishment, if she found out, would be excessively severe.

His interest aroused, Fabio pattered back into the library. He decided to stay up a little longer to see if there was a sequel to what he had just witnessed.

In the library, Dobi was asleep in a chair, their unfinished chess game still laid out before him. If he should suddenly awake and start his nocturnal prowling, there was a danger he might discover Imre's secret. And the news was sure to get back to the Countess. The obvious course was for Fabio to remain in the library. If Dobi was to awaken and make to leave, he would delay the Steward and save Imre from discovery.

Satisfied with his plan, Fabio slumped into the welcoming grip of his old armchair and eased his aching eyes shut. The castle was silent except for the swinging pendulum clock and Dobi's heavy rhythmic breathing.

An instant later, the bishop Dobi had been holding in his sleeping grasp clattered to the floor. Dobi started awake and looked about him.

Fabio had kept his eyes shut when the unexpected noise came. To Dobi's inspecting eye, the older man was peacefully asleep. At last, breathed Dobi. It was almost impossible to get the old man out of the library, so he would have to take his chance now, while he slept. Taking great pains to be quiet, Dobi rose and moved over to the book-shelves. He began to scan the shelves for a certain book.

Fabio raised half an eyelid and furtively peered out. He was surprised at what he saw. Dobi browsing among the books! It was almost unbelievable. He had never shown himself interested in literary matters before. And why were his movements so furtive? Something was definitely going on, decided Fabio.

As he watched, Dobi took down the book he was seeking and started to return. Fabio hastily closed his eyes tight.

Seeing the old man was still asleep, Dobi carried his prize to a desk, where a candle afforded some light. He sat down and began to flick keenly through the book. The pages were yellow and crumbling, but the words were still as legible as the day they had been laboriously copied down.

Fabio heard the rustling of the pages. Surprising himself with his bravery, he dared another look. Dobi was scanning an old book over by the desk. His fingers hid the title, but even as Fabio watched, Dobi moved a hand and Fabio read the words 'The Human Body'.

He closed his eyes and thought. That old thing! He recalled the book now. It was not the medical text the title suggested, but an alchemical work, a relic inherited from one of the Countess's necromancer ancestors. Was Dobi thinking of taking up sorcery? Fabio smiled to himself. That was probably it. Some village slattern had rejected him and the old bear was trying to woo her with the help of magic!

The explanation almost satisfied Fabio. Even so, he thought, a lot of unusual activity seemed to be taking place in the castle.

Imre and the young Countess were locked in a passionate embrace. All the pent-up frustration of the previous evening was released in a flood of desire. Ecstatically, the Countess rubbed her face against his, her hair streaming down over his shoulder. Their hands explored restlessly, frustrated by the presence of their constricting clothes. Imre hungrily pressed his lips to her hot open mouth and sucked her tongue. She trembled, gasping, in his arms as he teased her wriggling tongue gently with his teeth. His hand snaked up her eager body and grasped one of her firm breasts. Underneath her blouse, he could feel her nipple harden. The Countess shuddered, feeling the heat of his loins against her, his hardness rising.

Behind them, the violet-coloured bed waited invitingly. Without conscious effort, their bodies moved towards it. Imre, tortured by longing, wildly caressed her hair. He bent down, nuzzling her neck, kissing and biting her pale shoulders.

'Oh darling,' he whispered breathlessly... 'I thought the day would never end...Say you love me, say it!'

Her reply came like a moan of pleasure, 'Yes...Yes...I love you!'

Excitement stirred moistly through her body. She wanted him to throw her on the bed and plunder her aching flesh.

'And you'll never leave me?' he demanded, fumbling to undo her dress.

'Never, never, darling...' She flung an arm round his neck to hold him closer. As she did so, she caught sight of her hand, and what she saw froze her with horror. It looked yellow and dried up, an old woman's hand.

Turning from Imre, whose attention was still on her shoulder, she saw her reflection in the cheval mirror. Her wrinkles and hard lines had returned twofold. She looked older and uglier than ever before.

Wrenching herself violently from Imre's grasp, she ran sobbing to the door and out of the room, keeping her face well hidden. For a second Imre was rooted to the spot, stunned. One moment the girl was in his arms, as passionate and aroused as he was himself. The next, she had flown without a word of explanation. He cast a rueful glance at the bed and hurried after her.

In the corridor he stopped, helpless, as he caught sight of Ilona's slim figure disappearing into her mother's room.

In her room, the Countess ran to her dressing mirror, her stomach acid with fear. A glance was sufficient to confirm her worst fears. Her age had caught up with her in a terrible way.

The sight of her ugliness captivated her, forced her to approach the mirror and examine herself in fearful detail. Her pallid skin was pitted and crevassed; thick whorls of wrinkles were spun out across her face. Angry boil-like blemishes were sprouting on her chin and forehead.

With a hopeless cry of despair, the Countess fell back from the mirror.

'Julie, Julie,' she pleaded and began to sob.

Within seconds, Julie anxiously entered the room. The sight of her cringing mistress upset her efficient features, and tore a cry from deep inside her. The Countess made a pathetic macabre vision in the disturbed candlelight. Her ravaged face contrasted hideously with the sagging red velvet gown, that had earlier shown off her beauty. A pink ribbon hung pitifully in the mess of lifeless gray hair around her streaming face. 'Oh my poor child,' exclaimed Julie and hugged her mistress, comforting her like a little girl that has lost her doll.

The Countess's body shook against her, convulsed by uncontrollable sobbing. The tears fell wetly against Julie's matronly bosom.

'Oh Julie, send him away,' wailed the Countess. 'He must not see me like this...please...please...send him away from me!'

Her despair was total, absolute.

Very softly, Julie began to hum a lullaby to the strange trembling creature in her arms.

The arrival of a circus in the village was a matter for great rejoicing and festivity. The barefoot children scurried to and fro alongside the circus wagon, squealing delightedly as it rumbled into town. Their mothers lined the cobbled streets, waving and shouting welcomes, or dancing hilariously to the novel music of the barrel-organ.

It was only a small circus but, in Veres, even a small circus generated enough excitement to last ten years. The villagers strained against their neighbours in the crowd for a glimpse of the curious visitors and uttered shill cries of delight when they succeeded. There was a dancing bear, and gypsies and a woman with a beard as thick as a man's, and a little man no taller than a chair and another with strange clothes and skin the colour of burnt bread...And a woman so monstrously, quiveringly fat that the hungry peasants gasped out loud, marvelling at the mountains of food she must have devoured.

In front of the procession came a short busy man, dressed in bright red and black satin. Half his sharp-featured face was painted white and the other half red and he spoke through huge scarlet lips. Not for an instant did he stay still, but ran here and there and leaped and cavorted and turned cartwheels and spun somersaults until the villagers were giddy just looking at him. And the whole time, his voice reached out seductively with promises of strange sights yet unseen. It sang liltingly above the music and animal cries and excitement:

'Roll up, roll up, everybody! All the fun of the circus!... In the marketplace tonight...See the animals, lions, monkeys, camels...The Indian fakir walking on nails...The fattest woman in the world...Join in the gypsy dancing...All the fun of the circus!'

On the wagon two swarthy musicians, one wearing a fez, the other a turban, seized their violins and plunged into a fast, swirling gypsy dance tune. There were delighted cries from the spectators as four beautiful gypsy girls jumped down from the wagon and began to dance wildly to the music, their long black hair streaming behind them. On their feet they wore tiny bells which tinkled and sparkled as they kicked up their legs and when they spun round, their flared, embroidered skirts rose up in a flurry of petticoats and the menfolk roared their appreciation. The gypsies danced and leapt and kicked and gyrated and laughed and flashed their dark eyes and made the villagers feel what it was like to be young and free and call no man master.

The wagon reached the gates of the castle and pulled up, awaiting admittance. Behind it, Julie threaded her way through the happy crowd. The cheerfulness of the villagers touched her and she nodded warmly at passing children and their parents. She slipped out of the crowd and through the gate into the castle.

The sound of the incessant fiddles reached the Countess's bedchamber, but it required more than music to soothe her mood. Looking every day of her real age and more, she turned angrily to Dobi who stood before her with a resigned expression.

'Don't you want to see me young and happy again?' she demanded.

He regarded her with sardonic amusement.

'So you can make love to young officers?' he countered.

Furious, the Countess turned her back on him.

Dobi sighed, exasperated by her unreasonable temperament. He stepped forward and, clasping her shoulders in his powerful hands, he spun her round to face him. Skilfully applied cosmetics hid the more recent ravages to her proud features. She wore an elegant black dress spangled with delicate silver tracery.

Despite her wrinkles, she still possessed a mature attractiveness that appealed to Dobi. He looked her over with approval.

'I'd rather have you as you are than watch you parading like some slut from the whore-house. At least there's some dignity in old age,' he concluded.

His display of sincerity was entirely lost on the Countess. She wrenched herself free and strutted out of reach.

'You're cruel!' she accused. 'You've never loved me!'

Her words stung Dobi.

'Oh, yes. I've loved you!' he flung back. 'But can't you see what'll happen to you if you continue behaving like this? You'll go insane,' he warned. 'Or the bailiffs will take you and hang you!'

She turned and met his stare, eyes fierce with hatred and malice. 'If that should happen, don't forget you'll be there next to me,' she reminded him.

Julie's entrance broke the tension. The Countess hurried to her.

'Have you spoken to him?' she anxiously asked the nanny.

Julie's familiar smile was reassuring.

'Yes, my dear. He was not at all offended. I told him you left because you heard your mother calling, and he seemed most understanding.'

The Countess let out a cry of relief and joy. She flung her arms around the nanny and hugged her.

'Oh, dear sweet Julie!' The nanny patted her on the back soothingly, enjoying her mistress's relief. Dobi watched the two women cynically. The Countess was behaving like a love-sick schoolgirl, completely forgetting the dignity of her status.

'He sends his good wishes and hopes you will go riding with him tomorrow as you arranged.' The Countess disentangled herself from the nanny's arms, her joy ebbing away.

'Riding with him?' she asked worriedly. 'But how can I, looking like this?' She gestured towards her face. Julie was placid and silent, unable to answer.

The Countess turned anxiously to Dobi. He shook his head, ignoring her pleading look. She faced Julie once more.

'Julie, you will have to help me,' she said. 'Find me someone and bring her to me.'

Julie nodded. She knew it was not a request but an irrefutable order.

'Yes, Countess,' she acquiesced. 'But first, tell me, what news of the little one, our real daughter?' The nanny's face was tight with concern for Ilona.

The Countess turned sharply away, looking to Dobi for reassurance.

He remained grimly silent.

'I'm anxious,' continued Julie. 'She should be here by now.'

'But didn't Captain Dobi tell you, Julie?' asked the Countess, striving to sound composed.

'No.' Julie shook her head, her eyes fixed anxiously on the Countess.

'The Danube flooded where her coach was to have crossed,' said the Countess in a matter of fact voice that displayed no emotion. Julie hastily crossed herself and began to whine.

'Oh, my poor child!' she howled, as if the news had just arrived that Ilona was captured by the Turks.

'She is quite safe,' the Countess assured her as Julie continued to sob.

'Now, Julie,' reprimanded the Countess. 'Please do as I ask.'

Dobi interrupted, a warning in his voice.

'It cannot be anyone from the castle. The bailiffs are already asking questions.'

The Countess gnawed her lip. Having an outsider brought in would arouse too much curiosity.

Wiping her eyes, Julie went over to the window, attracted by the cheery gypsy music from the courtyard below. An instant later her eyes gleamed and she called out excitedly, 'Countess, come quickly. Look!'

The Countess hurried over to the window and peered out. The circus wagon, a confusion of over-bright colours, had entered the courtyard. A red-garbed clown was walking on his hands, inches ahead of the snapping jaws of curious dogs. The musicians with their strange headgear were still sawing feverishly at their instruments. The Countess's gaze fixed on a pretty, raven-haired gypsy girl. She was happily beating a tambourine as she twirled to the music.

The Countess looked up into Julie's dark insinuating eyes. 'Will the Countess have her fortune told?' Julie asked playfully.

The Countess looked down again at the twirling figure of the gypsy girl and nodded, smiling.

The Sergeant of the Bailiffs had a face like a black-bearded pig. The similarity was not lost on Hugo, the castle butcher, as he hacked and truncated a pig carcass with his cleaver.

The Sergeant was seated at a sturdy wooden table in the castle kitchen. His bulging eyes wandered greedily over the mountains of chopped vegetables before him and, above, the smoked hams, salamis and ripening game-birds that hung temptingly from the ceiling. His nostrils quivered, assaulted by a rich feast of odours. He found it exceedingly hard to keep his mind on his mission.

Around him clustered the castle servants, except for Hugo, whose cleaver rose and fell steadily, the slapping of blade against pig-flesh punctuating the Sergeant's words.

'And you've heard nothing from this Teri since?' he asked disinterestedly, helping himself to another glass of the Countess's excellent wine.

Concept / Art Direction — Nigel Wingrove
Photography — Chris Bell **Stylist** — Spencer Horne
Hair and Make up — Ashley Mae
Models: — Countess Dracula — Eileen Daly
Blond woman — Marie Harper **Gypsy** — Maria

In between sobs, Rosa, the cook, managed a reply.

'Two days she's been gone. And still no news of her,' she blubbered. Another cook, Anna, a skinny red-haired woman, leaned knowledgeably towards the Sergeant.

'If you ask me, the Countess knows what happened to her,' she offered.

'No one's asking you,' scowled the Sergeant, licking his lips at the sight of a huge gooseberry pie being taken out of the blazing oven.

Around him, Anna's words had stimulated a torrent of noisy accusations.

'Tell him how the old witch used to treat her!' cried Ilonka, the kitchen maid, above the others.

'Tell him how she used to burn and slap her!' A chorus of agreement climaxed her words.

'Quiet!' ordered the Sergeant, flaring his fat nostrils. 'You ought to be ashamed of yourselves! Show a bit of respect for the Countess.'

Ilonka laughed contemptuously.

'Why should we?' she snapped.

'For your food and the warmth of this kitchen and the guns of her soldiers that protect you from the rampaging Turks,' he angrily replied, jowls shaking. He seemed unaware of the jealousy his words betrayed.

The servants were so engrossed in his discourse that none of them turned at the sound of footsteps moving stealthily up the back stairs. If they had done, they might have witnessed an attractive gypsy being led up the steps by Julie.

'Ungrateful lot!' stormed the Sergeant at the servants. 'You're the envy of the village, you know that?' He glanced around them impressively, letting them feel his importance. 'So be satisfied, and keep your mouths shut,' he sternly concluded. The servants remained sullenly quiet, their previous rebelliousness crushed.

The only sound was the steady slap of Hugo's disembowelling cleaver. Then Rosa's wailing erupted again, forced out by the intensity of her distress.

'I just want someone to find my Teri, my little girl,' she bleated. 'I want to see her alive again!' She collapsed in an outburst of sobbing as Ilonka sat beside her and tried to comfort her in a soothing voice.

The Sergeant drank his wine to the dregs. Swilling the last of it contentedly around his mouth, he turned to Rosa and said, 'She'll turn up eventually. They always do. She's probably hiding out in the forest with some lusty lad.' He guffawed, his gross body shaking under the disapproving eyes of Rosa and the others. 'Anyway, how many other children have you got?' he asked, heaving himself out of the chair and making for the door.

'Seven,' replied Rosa piteously.

'Seven!' The Sergeant belched and laughed.

'Well, what are you worrying about? You won't know the difference anyway...' Still laughing and clutching his belly, he pushed past Hugo and eased his bulk out the door.

Watching him, Hugo picked up his sharpest cutting knife and ripped through the whole length of the pig's carcass with a noise like a tearing sheet.

In the Countess's salon, Julie and the Countess watched with unconcealed excitement as the gypsy girl laid out a succession of colourful Tarot cards before them. The girl examined each card carefully as if it divulged unfathomable secrets to her only. Her abundant black hair was secured by a band of copper rings around her forehead and, at every movement, she released the laughter of tiny golden bells. She was darkly beautiful and very mysterious.

The last card to be turned over bore a picture of a handsome knight with a feather in his cap. The gypsy gasped as if a particularly splendid prophecy had been revealed to her. 'I see a new love in your life,' she announced to the Countess who nodded approvingly, an eager smile on her face.

'He will lift away the black veil of your widowhood. You will be young in heart again,' she prophesied.

The Countess nodded again, as if the gypsy's revelations corresponded to what she herself had already deduced. She made a sign to Julie who left the room and returned a few seconds later carrying a richly ornate black box. The gypsy girl eyed the box curiously, wondering what sort of reward it would yield.

The Countess saw her interest as she took the box; she kept it tantalisingly closed.

'I promised I would cross your palm with silver,' she said.

Then she flicked open the box and lifted out a beautiful necklace. Pure silver, its brilliance danced temptingly in the Countess's hand. The girl murmured astonishment, overwhelmed by the Countess's generosity.

The Countess handed the box back to Julie and moved round behind the gypsy girl. Deftly, she slipped the girl's gaily embroidered blouse off her shoulders. A plump, brown breast slipped out. The Countess reached out and caressed the pretty breast, fingering the nipple that was strangely pink against the deeper tint of her skin. The girl turned and smiled at the Countess, an open invitation to do with her body as she wished.

The Countess draped the necklace around the willing girl's neck. The delicate workmanship sparkled brilliantly between her lush breasts.

'It's beautiful,' said the gypsy with awe.

Her hesitant hand reached up to touch the jewels.

As she did so, the Countess removed a long, pearl-topped hairpin from her greying locks, raised it above the girl's unsuspecting back and plunged it down into her neck. The girl gave a small cry of pain as the blood jetted from her punctured jugular vein. Her hand made a feeble effort to reach the pin and draw it out. The groping fingers never found it. She crumpled to the floor.

For a moment, the Countess stared down at the twitching body. Then she knelt down and began to wash her hands in the growing pool of softly spurting blood.

Imre was in his stables saddling the black stallion. The novelty of ownership had worn off and he felt thoroughly dejected. It was two whole days since he had seen Ilona and he was beginning to think she was avoiding him. How else could he have missed her in the secluded world of Castle Veres? It was doubly depressing since he had decided that she was the someone special he had been searching for. Every time he considered her matchless beauty, her wit and charm, he was certain that he had found the perfection he was holding himself back for. Their meeting, their mutual attraction, it all seemed divinely inspired. And now, he could not bear to be without her.

He heard a voice calling to him.

'Imre!'

There was no mistaking Ilona's sweet voice. He ran outside to meet her.

The young Countess smiled down at him from atop her white mare. She seemed even more beautiful than in his dreams. She wore a lambskin tunic of purest white, lovingly embroidered with blue designs and fragile gold needlework. A dainty black riding hat, circled with red ribbons and plumed with a blue feather, perched on top of her golden curls.

Imre hurried forward to help as she gracefully dismounted. Then they were locked in each other's arms, lips pressed together in a kiss that gripped them, tirelessly, in its passion.

At last, they separated, looked lovingly at one another.

'However can you forgive me for the other night?' she asked breathlessly with such a look of childlike despair that he seized her and kissed her again. When they drew apart, he said, 'Julie explained everything. Don't worry.' She smiled warmly at his understanding nature, and gave him a peck on the cheek for being so kind. Laughing, he took her hand and led her into the stable.

As he finished strapping the ornately stitched saddle to his mount, she watched him, finding perfection in every motion. 'How is your mother?' he asked concernedly, reflecting that he had not seen the old Countess for several days either. The young Countess sighed, apparently sharing his concern.

'A little better but still confined to her room,' she said. 'It must be the shock of my father's death. And then my homecoming.'

There was an awkward silence. Words were clumsy, ridiculous things that could never convey the intensity of their feelings. Passion stirred in their young bodies as they gazed at each other. They waited, smiling, for the inevitable. He could not bear to delay any longer. Impetuously, he caught hold of her and crushed her to him. Her eager body pressed itself to his and her nails dug into his back. As he sought her lips, he saw her eyes bright with desire.

'Ilona,' he cried, 'Love me...Love me...'

Her tongue snaked up his cheek, tickled his ear.

'Oh, yes...yes, my darling,' she whispered breathlessly. 'Oh, don't ever leave me!'

He pulled her down onto a pile of straw. They rolled over and over, moaning at each hot contact of their bodies. He lay on top of her, covering her face with uncontrollable kisses. His tongue flicked over the hard, white edges of her teeth and slipped into her mouth, stirring its warm wetness. She murmured soft encouragements as he fumbled with feverish haste at the buttons of her blouse. Her blouse gaped open and her breasts tumbled out, white and luscious. His mouth sucked in the pink berries, and he felt them stiffen under the affections of his tongue. He buried his head between her breasts, rubbing them with his untidy brown hair.

Her head rolled back and forth with growing frenzy as he pulled down her skirt and silken underwear, revealing her nest of golden down. Releasing his buttocks, her hands reached up and pulled her hairpin loose and flung it aside. She shook loose her blonde locks which flooded softly over his shoulder and between her taut breasts. Stroking his cheek with one hand, she reached down with the other and coaxed his stiffness, guiding it towards the centre of her desire. Imre lunged into her arching, shuddering body and found ecstasy.

Imre's senses were adrift, seemingly suspended in blinding sunlight. His thrusting body was driven by a turbulent atavistic spirit he had never known was in him. Only a fragment of his conscious mind was functioning and his vibrating nerves told him he had attained fulfilment. Perfection was his.

With cries of exhilaration, they dissolved into togetherness and knew irrevocably that they were one and would be together always and that neither could live without the other.

Ignored, forgotten beside the sheet of golden hair lay the Countess's hairpin. The same one that had been thrust into the gypsy girl's neck to release her lifeblood

In the lonely wood-cutter's hut by the edge of the forest, Ilona's heart beat anxiously as she watched Janco pause hesitantly in the doorway. Please, please let him go out, she prayed.

She had discovered that the walls of the hut were only thin clay and, in some places, the driving rain had almost washed the clay away. In the few moments when Janco was not watching her, she had managed to scoop out a small hole in the floor beside a wall where the clay was very thin. If Janco would only leave for a while, she could easily make a breach in the wall and crawl out to freedom.

As she watched, Janco turned to look her over once more. She smiled back as innocently as she could manage. Satisfied, Janco nodded his shaven head and stepped outside, shutting the door behind him. An instant later, she heard the key turn in the lock.

Her excitement growing, she waited a couple of minutes to let Janco get out of hearing distance. Then she began to redouble her efforts, kicking urgently at the weakened point with her pretty silver-buckled shoes.

Moments later, her efforts were rewarded and the hole was big enough to push her foot through. The breeze on her leg felt good. She pounded at the sides of the opening with her heel to enlarge it.

Outside the hut, Janco stared down at the little shoe as it was forced through the wall. Dropping to his knees, he seized hold of the shoe in both hands and, chuckling wildly, began to smother the slim ankle with kisses.

From the other side of the wall came a terrified scream and Ilona's foot was hastily withdrawn back into the safety of the hut.

Happy and laughing, Imre and the young Countess rode together beneath the trees. In their eyes, all of the green summer countryside seemed to reflect their own enchantment. Even when not speaking, they would glance at each other as if to reassure themselves that such complete happiness was not a fanciful dream but reality.

Coming to a pleasant spot on the bank of a river, they dismounted and tethered their horses to a bush. Then they lay down on the grassy bank and held hands, enjoying the peaceful solitude and the silvery reflections of the sun on the water.

The young Countess stretched out and closed her eyes, feeling the warmth of the sun play on her body. She had never felt such perfect contentment, she told herself. And now that she had achieved it, she meant to keep it. Her strong will had rebelled against cruel Fate which enslaved other humans - and she had triumphed.

A sudden feeling of unease made her open her eyes. A cloud was passing across the sun, cutting off its warmth. Then she saw that Imre was staring down at her with anxious concern. 'What's the matter?' she asked hurriedly, sitting up and pressing urgent hands to her face. Her skin felt silken soft. She had not lost her beauty after all.

'Nothing,' admitted Imre, smiling. 'I can't get used to my good fortune, that's all.' The Countess smiled with relief. Her secret was safe.

Imre examined a freshly-plucked daisy as he spoke. 'Two weeks ago,' he said, 'I was just another young officer with my unit. And now, here I am...a man of some means...'

He glanced at her admiringly.

'...With the most beautiful woman at my side.'

She laughed and hugged him and happily pulled him down onto the grass.

'I share your good fortune,' she said joyfully.

Despite her words, Imre's face clouded with sudden anxiety.

'But can you really love me?' he asked.

She looked at him.

'Of course I can. Why do you ask such a silly question?'

Imre shrugged.

'Because you're a young Countess, and I'm only the son of a soldier.'

'A very brave soldier,' pointed out the Countess. 'A General.'

'True,' admitted Imre, 'but I cannot trade on his reputation. I have my own way to make.'

Leaning over, he tickled the end of her pretty nose with a long blade of grass. She giggled enjoyably.

'And by your standards, I have much to learn,' he said.

'Then let me teach you,' she said seductively, disarming him of his blade of grass and taking him in her arms.

They kissed for several minutes. Finally Imre raised his head.

'My mistress...' he declared, '...and my master.'

The Countess pressed a chastening finger against his lips.

'No, you are my master,' she affirmed. 'And always will be.'

He seized her in his arms and kissed her passionately and soon they were unconscious of everything except the enjoyment of each other's bodies.

The day was warm and the women of the village were down by the river washing their laundry and pounding the wet clothes with rocks. It was also an excellent opportunity to share the latest gossip.

Their chattering died away as Grigory's widow, Maryska, walked up. She had looked worn and haggard since the still-born birth of their third child, but now she looked like a corpse. Her sunken eyes stared out fiercely above hollow cheeks and her dark hair hung in greasy strands. Until the death of her husband she had taken some care in her appearance. Now her clothes were soiled and reeking.

As she drew nearer, the women saw that she was talking to herself, her features animated as if she was taking part in an argument. Several of the younger women pointed two fingers in her direction to ward off the evil eye. The more faint-hearted got up and ran, their washing streaming wetly behind them. Maryska saw them leave and laughed, a harsh animal sound. Let them run, she thought. She did not need their sympathy. She did not need anybody.

A childless couple had agreed to look after her boys, Georgy and Sergei, and her own needs were small. She knew she did not have a pretty face anymore but she was inventive and her body was still good and soldiers and shepherds would pay a couple of kröner for its use. She could earn enough to live on until she found herself another man.

Maryska slumped down among the women squatting on the river bank. Most of them were old friends and they did not shrink away. Murdered husbands and temporary derangements were commonplace and, besides, this was an interesting break in the day's chores. The women gathered around her, shrunken, toothless faces jockeying for a better position.

Maryska scowled and pointed at the castle, towering blackly above the village. From the back of her throat, she dredged up a gob of spit and propelled it expertly into the frothing river. The women cackled their approval.

'Up there she sits, in her finery,' accused Maryska.

'She lost her man, so she took mine from me!' Her voice rose in a wailing screech that carried clear to the village.

'Devil woman! Devil woman!'

So loud was her outcry that her companions looked nervously around to see if the sound had attracted any bailiffs. None appeared and Maryska was able to continue with her story.

'Bad blood breeds rotten blood!'

Her black eyes prowled over her listeners, daring them to contradict. They nodded eagerly.

Appeased, Maryska raised her face to Heaven as if the history of the Bathory family was scrawled across the sky in blood.

'Her father died a cuckold twenty times over....Her uncle spoke with demons and was carried off to the flames of Hell by the Horned One.... Her brother was an adulterer and rapist who tore the skirts of nuns and gentlewomen....'

The washerwomen clucked like angry hens. They had heard these tales many many times, but they knew it was all true and worth retelling.

'Her aunt was cursed and could not lie with men, so she took others of her own sex into her bed,' sneered Maryska, warming to her subject.

'This Elizabeth, who is a friend to priests and bishops...' She paused to hawk up more spit which followed the same course as the other.

'...This Elizabeth smeared a girl with honey and left her for the ants to chew on. The girl's crime to deserve such a death?' she asked.

'She stole a pear!'

Around her, the women hissed their outrage and shook their fists towards the castle. Maryska held up a grimy hand and the hissing ceased.

'The devil woman has other kin.' she continued. The women were silent. They knew they were about to hear a juicy new morsel of scandal about the mistress of the manor.

'To the east rules a tyrant who is neither dead nor alive...who kills for love of blood.'

Maryska smiled to see them breathing the name, not daring to say it aloud. She leaned closer to her audience and her voice dropped to a whisper.

'Aye,' she said, 'our Countess is cousin to Dracula, the bloodsucker!'

The women crossed themselves energetically and cast frightened glances at the castle. Maryska cackled at the sight of their fear.

'Countess Dracula...' she whispered.

Jumping up, she swept her arm towards the black castle, her voice rising in a scream of hatred as she repeated the words - 'COUNTESS DRACULA!'

Fabio was descending the staircase to the main hall of Castle Veres when he saw something that excited his interest. Below stood Dobi, in conference with two of the most villainous characters he had ever set eyes on.

One was darkly tanned and wore a red bandana round his head in the manner of a gypsy. A gold ring flashed in his ear. His companion was a tall, heavily-bearded fellow with fierce black brows and looked the likely perpetrator of any misdeed imaginable. Dobi was counting gold coins into the palm of the black-bearded ruffian.

As Fabio watched, Dobi lifted his head and saw him. The appearance of a witness to his transaction seemed to speed up the conclusion of business, thought Fabio.

As Fabio reached the bottom of the staircase, Dobi dismissed the two men and ushered them out through a side door. Then he turned back to Fabio with a look of unusual amicability that did not quite hide his unease.

'What's your business with those two villains?' queried Fabio, staring after the fast-disappearing figures.

Dobi arched his grey brows as if astonished that the honesty of two such pleasant fellows could be questioned.

His ruse did not impress Fabio.

'Why, I saw them not two hours ago, creeping into the forest with a heavy load." he elaborated. 'To be sure they were carrying stolen loot or the body of some unfortunate traveller.'

Dobi laughed and slapped Fabio's back in cheerful reproach. Fabio winced at the pain stinging his back. He much preferred the quieter, less demonstrative Dobi he was accustomed to.

'But of course, they're friends of Janco, the game-keeper,' exclaimed Dobi with aggressive amusement. 'They take him his provisions. That's what you saw, my friend.'

'Oh, was it indeed?'

Fabio hurrumphed to indicate that such a story might satisfy the likes of Dobi, but it did not satisfy him for an instant.

'Yes, well...he must have a big appetite...an enormous appetite,' concluded Fabio.

Still laughing, Dobi moved to the table and poured two large mugs of ale. One of them he offered to Fabio.

'No, no,' refused the old scholar. 'It somewhat dulls my senses this time of day.'

'Come on, drink,' urged Dobi. 'Drink to the Countess Ilona.'

'Well, if you insist...'

Reluctantly, he accepted the mug and took a sip of the bitter brew. He grimaced, then pointed an accusing finger towards Dobi.

'And while we're about it, what's happened to Countess Elizabeth?' he demanded. 'She hasn't left her room for days. Isn't she ever going to show herself? And she can't be very sick or she'd have called for her physician...'

He knitted his white brows, puzzled at such an illogical situation.

'And I can't believe it's grieving widowhood that detains her,' he added wryly, braving a sly glance at Dobi which he hoped would suggest that he knew more than he did.

If he had hoped to precipitate an angry reaction which would disclose something new, Fabio was disappointed. Dobi stared sternly back at him, then threw back his ale in a single swig. He wiped his mouth with the back of his hand.

'What are you worrying about, Fabio?' he ridiculed. 'Isn't it a better place without her?'

With a last sharp look at Fabio he strode away and hurried up the stairs.

Fabio was not deluded by Dobi's earlier mock display of levity. More than anything, it left him convinced that something was going on without his knowledge. And he was determined to find out exactly what it was.

Imre's happiness was so complete, it felt unreal. Even the scarlet blooms in the rose garden appeared dream-like in the moon's rays. Hand in hand with the young Countess, he was walking through the courtyard towards the black mass of the castle tower.

It was as if he had cheated fate of its usual heavy tribute, he mused. Here he was, only twenty and already he was a battle-proven officer, wealthy, independent and the approved lover of one of Hungary's most desirable women. Most men took years to achieve just one of those ambitions and it left them worn and grey. Yet he had attained them all, without the loss of his youth.

Such knowledge sent a thrill of conquest through him. He knew he had been right to aim high, to save himself for the some-one special that his fellow officers had denied the existence of. He had proven them wrong. How jealous they would be when they heard of his good fortune, thought Imre.

It was important to him not to let success blind him to the demands of life. He now had to prove himself worthy of his luck. Instead of becoming self-satisfied and giving himself to excess, as others might do in his position, he would make good use of the extra time. His life would be one of carefully considered modera-tion, giving offence to no man. Neither lord nor serf would ever curse his name or have cause to complain of his actions.

Imre belonged to the new breed of men that believed even a peasant was a human being with a soul. He was anxious that, when himself a lord with a multitude of peasants under his dominion, he would not abuse his power but use it for the com-mon good. No, thought Imre, when he became a boyar, not even the lowliest peasant would tremble at his approach, or beg for work to feed his starving family.

But first, he had to secure his position. And make his love for Ilona acceptable in the eyes of God Almighty. He would do both by marrying her.

Imre and the young Countess had reached the door of the tower. They stopped and faced each other, neither anxious to end a day which was like the start of a wondrous new life.

Again Imre felt a slight panic as he looked into his love's eyes. They seemed so mature, so experienced for a girl of his own age. Their grey lustre seemed to suggest hidden depths of forbidden knowledge and Imre was again reminded of the sinister reputa-tion of her ancestors.

Quickly, he banished such thoughts by pulling her to him and kissing lips that withheld no secrets from him. At last, she lay her head on his shoulder and sighed contentedly.

'You've made me so happy, Imre,' she said.

'Then you'll marry me?' he asked, slightly surprised at hearing the words - as if they were spoken by someone else.

She took a step back, her tiredness shaken off by a new surge of delight.

'Oh, yes! Yes! Of course I will.'

And she threw her arms around him and held him tight.

'First I must talk to your mother,' said Imre, gently stroking her golden hair.

The young Countess shook her head and looked up at him with a smile of girlish enthusiasm.

'No, leave her to me.'

'Why?' asked Imre, an edge of anxiety in his voice. 'You fear she'll object?'

Ilona's laughter was adorable.

'Don't be silly. She likes you very much.'

A fleeting sadness passed through the young Countess's face as she added, 'But she's old and needs to be humoured.'

She quickly recovered herself and stood on tiptoe to plant a kiss on Imre's forehead.

'Do it quickly,' he urged. 'Speak to her tomorrow.'

'I will,' promised the Countess.

Imre gave her one final, lingering kiss and then started back along the path, excitement suddenly forcing his legs into a run. He turned back once and waved to her, before disappearing into the darkness.

The young Countess watched him go, then she entered the tower and began to climb the cold winding stairs to her room. As she climbed them, eerie shadows swirling around her, her youthful face was made long with apprehension and worry. It was the look of a much older woman.

The sun hardly penetrated the part of the forest where Sergei and Georgy were playing. The two boys crept through the shadows, the branches reaching out for them like witches' thin fingers.

Georgy squealed every time a bird flew up with sudden beating wings, or a squirrel scurried past. He had only vague recollections of his father, but he could vividly remember the terrifying stories that Grigory had told him about the wood. Stories about men who got down on all fours and turned into creatures that ripped and tore flesh and sat cracking the bones of children. Of sorcerers who trapped boys in cages and melted them into candles. And shadow-like vampires carrying clanking buckets to collect the blood of their victims.

Keenly Georgy scrutinised the tops of the trees for nests. They were seeking birds' eggs for the supper table. So far, they had only found three measly robin's eggs. If they returned home with nothing more substantial, they were sure to be whipped for their idleness.

He wondered where his mother was now. He had recently seen her in the company of a bad-tempered soldier. The soldier had shouted at the boys and cuffed them and Georgy no longer missed his mother like he used to.

Abruptly, Georgy became aware that he was alone. Sergei was gone. A coldness gripped him as he ran about, desperate for a glimpse of his brother. His shouts sounded small and weak in the vastness of the forest. He looked about in panic. Even the cries of the birds now sounded uncanny, like the cackling of the child-stealing sorcerer. Georgy imagined himself being lowered into the bubbling cauldron and began to shake.

Suddenly, with a horrible cry, a figure leapt out at him from the bushes.

Georgy shrieked.

'Aaaaagh! I'm the Vampire and I want your blood!' cried Sergei from behind bared fangs.

Georgy's wail of terror turned to an angry shout and deteriorated into laughter. He picked up some sticks from the forest floor and flung them at the older boy who ducked and ran, taunting, deeper into the forest, kicking up dead leaves as he fled.

Shouting excited threats, Georgy gave chase and they ran haphazardly through the densely packed trees. Georgy suddenly stopped, his fear and anger forgotten.

'Look, there's a good'un! Up there!' he shouted, pointing to one of the lower branches of an old oak. Sergei looked and saw a bird's nest crouched on the branch. It looked big and promising.

'I'll get it!' cried the older brother and he started to climb the tree with monkey-like expertise. It looked like a magpie's nest and Sergei hopefully wondered if it would be full of jewels like in the stories he had heard.

An instant later, he cried out as a small branch snapped under his weight and he fell, a tangle of arms and legs, into the piled-up leaves.

The fall was not as bad as he had anticipated. He had been waiting to feel the scraping pain of dry earth under the leaves. Instead, he could feel something cold and pliable beneath his hands and knees. He thought briefly of when he had touched his dead father's hand and found, not fatherly warmth but goose-pimpling coldness.

Then he was busily scattering leaves to see what lay underneath. When he saw, he screamed and his brother echoed his terror in a shrill voice.

Beneath the clinging leaves lay the naked body of a beautiful girl with black hair. She looked like a gypsy except that her dark skin was horrifyingly tinged with blue. There were vivid red slashes at her throat and wrists and her whole body seemed emptied of blood.

'It's the Vampire! He's got her!' howled Georgy.

And then he was racing across the forest for the safety of the village and his brother was not far behind.

In her bedchamber, the young Countess pushed away her heaped luncheon plate. It was not good for her complexion, she thought, to eat pig-flesh. She picked up a ripe pear and bit daintily into it, waiting for Dobi's anger to reach a crucial point. She had just announced her intention of marrying Imre.

Behind her, Dobi suddenly paused in his pacing and glared at her in disbelief.

'Married?' he scoffed. 'You're insane. You can't go on killing forever.'

The Countess's attention was riveted to the singularly juicy pear.

'Why not?' she asked. 'When I have you and Julie to help me.'

Dobi let her see his angry scepticism.

'And what about Fabio and the servants?'

The Countess turned to him in amazement.

'Surely you don't fear Fabio?'

'He's not such a fool as he makes out,' warned Dobi, recalling Fabio's questions about the two outlaws.

'We're quite safe,' said the Countess, returning her attention to the pear.

'And I'm happy,' she added. 'Or am I to understand you begrudge me even that small pleasure?'

Dobi glared at her for an instant, then strode to the door, flicking his black riding crop irritably against his leg.

'Where are you going?' demanded the Countess in a voice that made him stop. When he turned, there was a small ugly smile on his face.

'To meet your fiancé,' he purred.

The Countess raised her brow questioningly. Dobi was quick tempered and enormously strong. And he had no mercy for those who crossed him.

'It's perfectly all right,' he assured her, pleased to see she had sensed a threat in his words. 'We're signing the deeds of his inheritance. So I'll have the pleasure of his company tonight.'

He managed to make it sound like he was depriving the Countess of considerable pleasure. He opened the door and started to leave. Again, the Countess's voice stopped him.

There was authority in her voice as she said, 'Tell him the

Countess Elizabeth approves of our marriage.'

She tossed the carcass of the pear away from her with a triumphant flourish.

'And has made you responsible for the arrangements,' she concluded, knowing this was the surest way to humiliate her disappointed suitor.

Dobi slammed the door furiously and took several steps towards her.

'To Hell with the Countess Elizabeth!'

She laughed at his impotent rage, hushed him with a disapproving finger.

'Sssh...don't be so angry. I haven't forgotten you, I promise.' The last words were full of sensuous enticement. He regarded her silently, anxious for the promise to be fulfilled.

Slowly, she rose from her gilded armchair and walked towards him in a way that made him achingly aware of all the soft charms of her rejuvenated body.

Leaning forward, she planted a quick kiss on his lips and let him momentarily feel the warmth of her breasts against his chest. It was more than he could bear and he crushed her to him in his powerful grip. His lips pressed wetly over hers.

It was like a rapist's kiss, thought the Countess. Not the kiss of a young, inexperienced lover but the brutal, forceful insistent kiss of a man accustomed to kissing the drunkest whores. She saw his cold, warrior's eyes shone with lust. Her own urges stirred moistly and for a moment, she found she could not resist. Her body wanted to surrender itself to the thrusting assaults of this muscular, experienced plunderer.

Then her willpower reasserted itself and she broke out of his grip and skipped away from him.

'No, Dobi. Not now,' she said, like a mother withholding a sweetmeat from a pleading child.

'When?' he demanded, his broad chest heaving with frustration.

'Soon'

'Tonight?' His voice was insistent and she knew if she delayed too long, she would no longer be able to control him. Besides, it was so long since she had tasted his sinewy body.

'If you wish,' she consented, aroused by his eagerness. To Dobi, her laughter was both humiliating and exciting. Still, he was going to get what he wanted.

Grinning, he swaggered out of the room.

Georgy and Sergei watched excitedly as the Sergeant of Bailiffs and two of his men carried the gypsy girl's body out of the forest and loaded it into a cart that lay waiting on the muddy track. It made them feel important to know that they were responsible for all the excitement, to feel the eyes of the horrified villagers on them.

The Sergeant threw a red blanket over the bloodless body and turned to face the cluster of peasants, his piggy eyes boring into them as if weeding out the guilty party. The villagers shifted uneasily under his gaze, knowing that the Sergeant could make his life easier by simply accusing one of them and getting it over with. And no one would help them if he did.

'Any of you lot seen her before?' he growled.

The surly villagers shook their heads and murmured among themselves about vampires, ogres and werewolves. They voiced their ridiculous fears with such sincerity that the Sergeant spat disgustedly and told them to be quiet. He didn't need to ask twice.

'Are there any gypsies around here?' he asked loudly.

Hesitantly, a young man in a ragged, black sheepskin pushed his way to the front of the crowd.

'I've seen a few girls like her with the circus,' he announced. 'In the marketplace, last night. Why don't you go and ask them?'

His voice suggested that he and the others would be glad to see the Sergeant gone, the quicker the better.

The Sergeant glared at the youth as if he had just confessed to the crime. Finally, he looked away and said to no one in particular, 'It's probably one of these hot-blooded gypsies that did it. They're always fighting over their women, they are.'

He signalled to the cart-driver to get going. Then he eased his fat body onto the back of his protesting horse and he and his men rode away under the sullen stares of the peasants.

Janco was pouring himself a mug of ale when he heard the sound of horsemen approaching up the rough path that ran beside the hut.

Ilona heard it too because she made a sudden dash for the door. She tried to scream, but when she opened her mouth, Janco stuffed his big fist in it. She bit down savagely and he grunted but did not remove the flesh and blood gag.

Ilona struggled desperately, maddened by the awareness that possible deliverance was approaching just a few yards away. But she was tired with sleeplessness and weakened by hunger and her morale was almost as tattered as her clothes, and Janco easily pinned her down with his massive embrace.

Hastily, he picked her up like a child's rag doll and carried her under one arm to a large trunk in a corner of the rubbish-strewn hut. He dumped her in, upside down, and slammed the heavy lid and locked it. A muffled cry came from inside the trunk but it was not loud enough to carry outside.

Janco clapped his fur cap onto the greasy dome of his head and hurried outside to investigate. He paused to lock the door before starting down the track.

Coming towards him was a grim procession of horsemen and a cart. There seemed to be something covered by a blanket on the cart but Janco paid it no attention. He was too terrified by the sight of the Sergeant of Bailiffs riding at the head of the procession.

The Sergeant gave him a suspicious, searching look, and urged his horse towards the grotesque figure of the large bald mute. Janco backed resentfully away and placed himself against the door of the hut, as if guarding it.

The Sergeant eyed him wearily.

'All right, all right. I'm not arresting you,' he said impatiently, peering down from his horse.

'Unless you've got a murderer in there...'

His bulging eyes roved over the hut in a way that made Janco tense, ready to grab the lovingly-honed knife from of his boot and stick it in the Sergeant's fat gut.

The Sergeant appeared to lose interest in the hut and turned back to Janco.

'Have you seen anyone with a gypsy girl going into the forest?'

Janco shook his head, aggressively helpful.

The Sergeant dismissed him with a grunt and spurred his horse on up the track. Behind him, the procession resumed its journey towards the village.

When it was out of sight, Janco quickly unlocked the door, entered and relocked it from the inside. Then he shambled over to the trunk and opened the lid. Ilona emerged, breathless and filthy. Anxiously, she leapt out of the trunk and ran to the locked door.

She could no longer hear the sound of horsemen. The forest was quiet except for the unfriendly cries of birds and, presently, the sound of Janco guzzling ale and laughing in his peculiar tongueless manner.

The only place in the village of Veres where a good time might be bought was the Shepherd's Inn. Since, in general, the villagers had no coin to spare, they gathered outside and enjoyed the faint strains of music they could not see being played. For those with a jangling purse, however, and a taste for full-bodied wine, strong ale and spicy goulash, the smoke-filled, noisy interior of the inn was a regular meeting place. And more fleshly tastes were catered for too, as was confirmed by the presence of numerous girls, with alluring bodies and provocative eyes. Their customers were the nucleus of the inn's regulars - local tradesmen and soldiers, successful brigands and, proving that greed is stronger than patriotism, a number of Turkish merchants. The latter generally sat in an exclusive fat-bellied group, smoking aromatic drugs in long-stemmed pipes and enduring the caresses of the resident girls, while wishing for the more refined attentions of their own harems. This particular night the regulars were supplemented by some of the circus performers and a party of travelling monks, who were bestowing some distinctly worldly attentions on the giggling ladies of the inn.

CHAPTER EIGHT

The door opened and Dobi stepped inside, followed by Imre. Almost magically, conversation and song died away and all heads turned in their direction. Unmoved by the sullen stares of the customers, the Steward of the castle led his young companion through the silent crowd to an empty corner table. As they sat, the sounds of revelry resumed, though noticeably subdued.

Imre felt uncomfortable at the hostile glances directed towards them. Having heard of the inn's notoriety, he had been looking forward to the evening, but the unwelcome reception suggested a disagreeable few hours ahead.

'Why do they stare at us so?' he asked Dobi.

Dobi looked about with open contempt, causing their antagonists to avert their eyes.

'Fear.' he answered, smiling in his sardonic fashion.

'Fear? Of what?'

Dobi shrugged as if it was only to be expected.

'As the dog fears its master,' he explained.

Imre laughed and shook his head. He had noticed a number of serving wenches and waiters, but none seemed keen to venture near their table.

'But a dog is also keen to serve its master. I fear we have no service,' he observed.

Dobi gave him a wry smile and thunderously clapped his hands, imposing an instant of silence on the entire gathering.

'You! Boy!' he bellowed, singling out a nervous young waiter hovering nearby.

'A flagon of wine. Speed!'

The youth hurried away as if the hounds of hell were upon his trail.

Imre smiled with appreciation at Dobi's ruthless handling of the situation and looked about him. There were a number of attractive girls on whom debauchery had left its mark in the form of sullen, sneering faces and lifeless eyes. Further away, across the room, he noticed a group of performers from the travelling circus: a clown, a bearded lady and two midgets.

All four looked towards him and Dobi with an evident dislike that Imre found both disturbing and inexplicable.

Imre turned to see that the nervous waiter had returned and was setting a flagon of thick red wine and two glasses before them. Dobi laughed contemptuously.

'You see? The pup obeys.'

He grasped the flagon from the boy's trembling fingers and filled both glasses.

Imre took a satisfying sip of wine and looked questioningly at Dobi.

'Does the castle command so much respect?' he asked setting down the glass.

'It commands. That's all that counts.'

Imre nodded. 'Then I, too, will soon command.'

It was a statement, not conjecture. Startled, Dobi looked up at him, through narrow inquisitive lids.

'By marrying the Countess Ilona,' Imre explained.

It took a short time for Dobi's delight to appear.

'The Countess Ilona!' he roared. 'Of course, let's drink to that!'

They clinked their glasses together and downed them both to the dregs.

Imre looked up to find that Captain Balogh, the chief Bailiff, was making his way through the chattering crowd. Striding up to their table, he flung some documents, decorated with heavy seals, onto the table in front of Imre. 'There you are, Lieutenant,' he said, 'signed, sealed and delivered. You are now the undisputed possessor of thirty-four horses and fifty-nine mares.'

As Imre excitedly examined the documents, Balogh's beefy red face caught sight of the flagon of wine and he emitted a little grunt of interest. Inviting himself to sit, he snatched an empty glass from a neighbouring table and helped himself to a goodly quantity of Dobi's wine. Dobi watched him coldly but said nothing.

Putting down his glass, Balogh turned to address Imre. 'What will you do with all these damn horses, make a gift of them to my good friend, the Captain here?' He shot a conniving look at Dobi.

'Or stay on in these parts?'

Imre grinned at Dobi.

'I have excellent reasons for staying on,' he said.

Balogh noticed the secretive look shared by his two companions. His interest aroused, he looked to Dobi for elaboration.

'The boy believes himself to be in love,' responded Dobi, with a trace of amusement.

Balogh looked askance at Imre.

'May I ask with whom?'

'It's no secret,' replied Imre. 'The Countess Ilona.'

'They're to be married,' added Dobi, without emotion, staring into the murky depths of his glass.

Surprise creased Balogh's brow.

'Has she returned?' he asked thoughtfully. 'I didn't know.' Leaning over, he pumped Imre's hand enthusiastically. 'My dear fellow, my heartiest congratulations!'

It seemed like a good moment for a drink, so all three glasses were filled and rapidly emptied again.

Behind them, a murmur of interest greeted the entrance of the Sergeant of Bailiffs. His harassed expression mad e it clear that his was a professional visit. He squeezed his bulk between the closely packed chairs and eventually reached Captain Balogh. Breathlessly he addressed him.

'It's the missing gypsy girl, sir. We've brought her back. She's in a horrible state.'

He paused and looked at all three of them, waiting for the best moment before announcing: 'Her blood's all gone!'

'Gone?' cried Balogh incredulously. 'What are you talking about? Explain yourself, man!'

The Sergeant's jowls quivered at the sound of his superior's reproachful voice. He injected an element of fear into his revelations to make them sound more important.

His low, throaty baritone sounded sepulchral as he said, 'Drained out of her, sir. Blue she is. The villagers...well, they're terrified.'

He hesitated for a moment, as if not sure whether to repeat the next bit of information. Finally he said,

'There's talk of vampires, sir!'

'Vampires?' guffawed Balogh, falling back in his chair, laughing.

'Ye Gods! Whatever will they think of next?'

Imre's reaction was one of interest, rather than amusement. 'Who do you think killed this girl?' he asked, hoping that Dobi would be able to make a suggestion based on broader experience. Dobi did not reply. He was staring stonily ahead, wrapped in his own thoughts. Seeing this, Imre turned to Balogh for his opinion. 'Some local lunatic,' asserted the bailiff knowledgeably. 'We'll soon have our hands on him.'

He looked up as one of the whores approached the table, and added quickly with a nudge for Imre -

'And here's someone we'd rather have our hands on!'

The others joined in his merriment, except for the Sergeant, who felt, with good reason, that his information was not being taken seriously.

The newcomer was a ripe blowsy blonde and her imminent arrival was preceded by a spectacular pair of breasts, that were as firm and luscious as watermelons. The flamboyant cleavage of her red silk dress provided an excellent opportunity to view these fine specimens. She was easily the most eye-catching of the whores at the inn.

'Ah, Ziza,' welcomed Balogh, motioning the sergeant aside and draping an arm around Ziza's ample rump, 'my dandelion...upholder of my throbbing dreams...my cathedral of flesh...' He broke off his testimonial to ask, with a sly look at Dobi, 'You've met the good Captain?'

Ziza glanced coyly at Dobi, as only a woman who has been in her line of business for fifteen years can.

'He's not so good,' she testified. 'I've made his acquaintance.'

Dobi chuckled to himself without looking up.

Balogh laughed his dirty laugh.

'But here's an acquaintance you haven't made,' he said. 'Lieutenant Imre Toth, who stands but an inch away from marriage - to a lady of noble birth.'

He held up two fingers of his right hand and let the forefinger of his left hover suggestively near the. This action brought about a peal of laughter that was dominated by the tempestuous Ziza.

'They'll make a fine pair,' added Balogh.

'But not as fine a pair as these, eh?' asked Ziza huskily, grinding her overwhelming bosom into Imre's ear.

The heady wine had made Imre more exuberant than usual. He reached out and patted Ziza's breasts appreciatively.

'The lady has a sizzling wit,' he said fondly. 'I'm in love with her already.'

'Her wit is not the only thing that sizzles' promised Balogh, groping his hand under her skirt.

'Here, feel the furnace...dip your finger into her liquid fires.'

Braying with laugher, he pushed Ziza towards the young officer.

She resisted, fluttering her long lashes with the modesty of a teasing virgin.

'Shame, Captain...I have my reputation to think of!'

'Indeed she has,' agreed the Bailiff, pressing his hands into her warmly yielding buttocks, intimating that her reputation might not be founded on the firm rock of chastity. He caught sight of one of the monks staring at them wide-eyed.

'And there's none sweeter in the whole province,' he added maliciously. 'She makes the prayer beads drop from a friar's thumbs.'

'And bulges men's pockets as she empties them,' testified Dobi.

They all burst into loud gusty laughter, the wine rendering them uninhibited.

When the hilarity had died down, the Sergeant uncomfortably cleared his throat to remind Balogh of his continuing existence. Balogh looked irritably up at him.

'What is it, Sergeant?' he demanded.

The Sergeant cast an embarrassed glance at Dobi, then leaned forward and whispered something into Balogh's ear, indicating that he could not talk openly in the present company.

Balogh rose, pursing his lips in annoyance.

'My watchdog calls,' he explained. 'Excuse me, gentlemen.'

He bowed briefly towards Dobi and Imre and turned to go, pausing to whisper in Ziza's ear,

'I'll be back!'

Ziza shrugged, suggesting he could please himself, there were plenty of other customers about. As if to corroborate this, a cry of 'Ziza, Ziza! Where are you, sweet one!' went up from a group of Turks on the other side of the room. She blew a kiss at Imre, then disappeared into the crowd. Dobi replenished Imre's glass with the last of the flagon, then signalled to the waiter for more. The boy scurried to obey.

Balogh and the Sergeant were forcing their way through the throng towards the door. In passing, the Sergeant nodded familiarly to the surly-faced clown and his companions. The clown responded with a wave that was almost a mocking salute.

When they had reached a position that was out of the hearing of the other customers, Balogh turned to the Sergeant.

'Yes?' he said, keeping an eye on Imre and Dobi at the back of the room.

'The victim, sir,' replied the Sergeant in a low significant tone.

'What about her?'

The Sergeant pointed towards the circus people.

'She's part of the circus. Went missing yesterday. One of her friends saw her going into the castle.' He lowered his deep voice emphatically. 'But nobody saw her come out.'

Balogh stared thoughtfully at Dobi, who seemed to be behaving with unusual friendliness towards the young Lieutenant.

'Proves nothing,' he said at length, turning back towards the Sergeant. 'I don't see why the castle should be involved.'

This remark did nothing to allay the Sergeant's suspicions.

'No, quite, sir. But all the same...' he began dubiously, then withered under his superior's gaze.

'All right, Sergeant, leave it to me,' said Balogh. 'I'll go up there later in the week and have a look around. Now take me to this bloodless corpse of yours,' he added as they stepped into the refreshing coolness of the night.

Without emotion, Dobi watched Balogh leave. He was not at all disturbed by the Sergeant's obvious suspicions concerning the castle. Countess Elizabeth was a powerful aristocrat with important relatives. Her status placed her almost above the law. That bumbling fool Balogh would never take action against her, thought Dobi confidently. Not unless the evidence was utterly conclusive. Cheerfully, he poured himself and Imre another glass from the new bottle. As they raised the wine to their lips, enthusiastic cries from the rowdier customers made them look up.

A dusky belly dancer streaked into the room on bare feet.

'Ah, Babouche, my love,' cried Dobi, raising his glass to her in a friendly toast. The dark beauty flashed back a pearly smile of recognition and then threw herself into her act as two squatting Turks began to play on flute and drums.

Sinuously, she writhed her ample body in time to the wailing oriental music, her fur-edged dress of gossamer veils streaming behind her. Golden bells danced between her fingers and her feet rhythmically pounded the wooden floor.

The customers leered and clapped, their faces wet with anticipation and a thick alcohol sweat. They shouted bawdy encouragements and pawed at her tanned flesh as she weaved tantalisingly in and out between the tables. Babouche tossed back her cascade of black hair and flared her nostrils proudly in mock rage, exciting her admirers to coarser suggestions.

She snaked in and out of the crowd, undulating her rolls of well-oiled brown flesh. Her stomach muscles swayed and throbbed in a shameless ritual of enticement. As she danced, she pulled away her covering veils one by one and threw them like nets of enchantment over her admirers. Each unveiling provoked louder cheers and enthusiastic clapping.

Unnoticed in the sweaty uproar, the sharp-faced clown left his companions and, clutching a basket of wares, began to edge towards Dobi's table with ferret-like movements. He was not wearing his pasty make-up, yet the look of cool arrogance sat rigidly on his face like a mask. As he passed a fat snoring Turk, he snatched the sleeping merchant's turban and placed it on his head, giving himself the appearance of a Moslem streetseller. He pressed nearer the unsuspecting victims of his attention.

With a flourish, Babouche cast the ultimate veil from her and stood revealed before their eyes, naked except for a fringed belt around her waist and two tasselled tips cupping her breasts. The customers surged forward; groping hands reached out to explore her substantial charms. Laughing aloofly, Babouche darted away from them and disappeared behind a curtain, precipitating cries of disappointment and thunderous acclamation.

Aroused by the spectacle, flushed with the heady wine, Imre was on his feet, clapping wildly. Dobi watched him cynically. He had seen Babouche's routine too many times, had explored her body too often for the dance to hold any mystery for him. Reaching out, he filled Imre's glass to the brim. Into his own, he poured only a fraction as much. Tonight was his night of love with the young Countess and he did not wish to spoil it by drinking away his potency or falling into a stupor.

Imre sat down, his eyes bright with excitement. Leaning back, he noticed Ziza staring intently at him from the bar and he flushed. Dobi did not fail to notice his reaction.

'You want her?' he asked, leaning confidently across the table.

Imre feigned surprise.

'Me? Ziza?' He laughed at the notion. 'No, she's for you, my friend. Your need is greater.'

There was a taunt in his voice that angered Dobi, but he did not show it. Still smiling, he wryly answered, 'Not tonight. You have greater need of her tonight.'

Uncertain of his companion's jibe, Imre looked puzzled.

'But I'm spoken for,' he said, dazed from too much wine.

Dobi watched with keen amusement as Imre picked up his glass and drank another mouthful.

'Tell me, Dobi,' he began, setting his glass down, and addressing the older man like a life-long friend, 'I'm curious to know...a man of your standing and authority...'

He paused briefly, having difficulty in fitting words together. 'Why have you never married? Don't you believe in it?'

Dobi shrugged indifferently. 'It fits some people.'

Imre clasped hold of Dobi's hand urgently, as if possessed by a sudden, brilliant idea.

'I think you should marry Countess Elizabeth!' he announced.

'She's free and...' - with a knowing smile -'...well seasoned ...a comfort and company for your old age.'

He raised his voice, captivated by his own splendid idea. 'We shall have a double wedding! Will you drink to that?'

He raised his glass and drank deeply.

Dobi regarded him ruefully. The young whelp was scratching too near the truth for his liking.

'Why should a man be a slave to one woman, when he can take his pick of many?' he asked.

He gestured to the whores hovering like predatory birds on the edges of the room. Neither Dobi nor Imre noticed the sharp-faced clown, who had sidled up to their table and was listening.

'Ah, but if one woman embodies all the desirable virtues...' started Imre, thinking of the many times he had had this discussion with his fellow officers in similar smoky dens.

Dobi sniffed scornfully.

'Mistress...friend...mother...all rolled up in one attractive package? Does such a woman exist?'

'You know she does,' replied Imre avidly. 'And I have found her.'

'Then you are blessed indeed,' said Dobi, looking away and drinking quickly to hide his displeasure.

'But also vulnerable!' taunted a high-pitched voice from nearby. Dobi and Imre turned to see the ferret-faced clown standing by their table. Imre laughed pleasantly.

'How so, Master Clown?' he asked.

The clown's voice was fast and flowery.

'Being so blinded by the light of your love, that you cannot see a man steal upon you under cover of the dark.'

Before these curious words had time to sink in, the wily clown had placed his basket upon the table and was raking through a strange assortment of trinkets. He dredged up a handful of gleaming black beads.

'Will you buy some beads - or a Turkish dagger to protect you from your enemies?'

He thrust forward a curved dagger, sparkling with gems, and held the evil-looking point towards Dobi, who regarded it coldly.

'Why should I have enemies?' asked Imre, sensing a serious intent behind the fellow's jest.

The clown watched him with crafty eyes.

'All men have enemies,' he softly warned. 'But blessed men more, since they are envied.'

Dobi turned to the clown, irritably pushing away his knife-wielding arm.

'That's Turkish talk. Away with you,' he ordered.

The clown held his stare with a sly knowing look. Then, smiling to himself, he placed the dagger back in the basket and asked Imre -

'Will you have your fortune told?'

As he spoke, he produced some large decoratively-painted Tarot cards.

'Yes...yes...read my fortune,' urged Imre enthusiastically. 'Tell me what the cards promise....'

With practised movements, the clown spread five cards on the table before them. He consulted them intently, mouthing his findings in a hushed voice.

'I see a wedding...and dragon's teeth...and a cruel woman...and..,' his eyes darted accusingly towards Dobi, 'the body of a hapless girl!'

Angrily, Dobi swept the cards from the table with one massive arm.

'Away fool! Away, I said,' he shouted threateningly.

The clown backed away and knelt quickly to retrieve his cards. A moment later, he stood up, presented an insolent bow and slunk away through the crowd to rejoin his strange companions.

There was a heavy silence between Dobi and Imre. Imre had been enjoying the jester's antics and resented Dobi's ill-treatment of the clown. What could the clown have meant? he puzzled. The dragon's teeth were surely those on the Bathory's coat-of-arms. And who was the cruel woman? Countess Elizabeth? The episode had sobered him.

'I recognise him,' said Imre thoughtfully, cutting through the unease. 'He's the clown from the circus. He talks of his gypsy girl.'

'For whom we grieve,' replied Dobi, brightening as he refilled their glasses. Imre watched him drink, again not knowing whether the Captain was making fun of him or not. He lifted his own glass and drank and, immediately, the searing liquid had him laughing again.

Dobi caught sight of Ziza lounging nearby, surrounded by admirers. Cheerfully, he waved her over. The buxom blonde approached the table.

'Me, Captain?' she pouted, touching a well manicured finger to her full lips.

'Yes, Ziza.' He nodded towards Imre.

'My young friend here is much taken with you.'

Imre smiled at the tart, not wishing to contradict the Captain. She smiled at him fondly, obviously approving of his good taste, and flopped herself down on his lap. Disconcerted, Imre laughed as Ziza put one arm around him and ruffled his hair with the other.

'No, no,' he protested to Dobi, Ziza shrieking with pleasure as he spilled his drink. 'She's yours...you take her!'

'Come on, man,' exhorted Dobi. 'Enjoy her while you still have the chance.'

He winked suggestively, hinting at the pleasures the busty Ziza could avail a man.

'What's the matter?' Ziza asked Imre in a motherly voice. 'Thinking of your lady love, are you?'

Breezily she thrust her bosom into his face.

Imre found himself helpless with drink and uncontrollable laughter. He burrowed his head between the soft, creamy peaks and shook with mirth.

The young Countess was brushing her hair before her dressing table. The golden locks shone sleekly beneath the brush strokes. She smiled at the reflected image of her beauty. She knew she had never looked so beautiful.

Suddenly her heart leapt as she saw the brush was clogged with gold threads of hair. She tried a few more vigorous brush-strokes and watched, gaping, as a bald patch of pink skin was revealed in the glow of the candles. Her remaining hair slithered from her scalp, as if powered by a terrible life of its own. She was left completely bald.

Helpless, horrified, tormented by a greater pain than any cutting blades could inflict, she watched as her skin flaked off in dry chunks. Her teeth fell from her mouth and tinkled onto the dressing table. The Countess's screams of agony gurgled and died in her tongueless mouth as the last shreds of flesh shrivelled and fell...

Fascinated, she stared into her reflection. The mirror showed her sitting in her high-backed chair in a purple velvet gown, her brush still gripped in a white-knuckled hand, perfectly normal.

Except that on top of the white ruffed collar squatted a fleshless skull, leering toothlessly back at her! And from her eye sockets blazed two lustrous hellish orbs, whose every movement matched those of her own eyes...

With a cry of terror, the young Countess sat up in bed, her face beaded with a fearful sweat. Her hands sprang to her face, feeling for signs of ageing, of decay. There were none and a gasping sigh of relief escaped her. Her terror had been a product of her own imagination. She gazed about the room, which was lit by the glow of a single candle. Everything was in order, there was nothing to fear. She was still young.

Nervously, she settled back onto the pillows. She closed her eyes but sleep evaded her. The moaning of the strong wind and the rattling of her open window trapped her in a state of alert consciousness. She wished that Dobi would arrive and love her to sleep in his muscular arms. Dismayed, she climbed from the bed and made for the open window. The wind rustled through her hair, making her shiver in her flimsy nightdress. Through the window, she could see the moon, an angry Cyclop's eye.

As she reached out to close the offending window, she caught sight of her reflection in the pane. The sight made her moan with horror and fall back towards the bed.

This time it was no dream. She was no longer the beautiful Ilona, but the bent and mouldering Countess Elizabeth.

At the Shepherd's Inn, bawdy excitement prevailed as the evening came to an end. The customers had swilled as much drink as they could stand and now they were preparing for a night of debauchery. Hard-faced whores, with softer bodies, furtively displayed their goods.

Customers expressed satisfaction, transactions were concluded, money exchanged hands and couples began to weave their way drunkenly to the upstairs rooms and the luxury of their plush, springy couches.

Imre was hardly aware of these developments. He was now so drunk his mind could only grasp one detail at a time, and that with difficulty. Beside him Ziza roared with throaty laughter at the antics of some of her fellow ladies of pleasure across the room. She waved to them and Dobi took advantage of the distraction to lean over and whisper something to Imre. The proposition made Imre roar with laughter and rock precariously on the back legs of his chair.

Ziza turned to find the source of amusement.

'What's the joke?' she asked the laughing men. 'Well, come on, let me in on it,' she coaxed, stroking the inside of Imre's leg.

Imre was helpless with hilarity and she turned impatiently to Dobi.

'I've made a bet with him,' the Steward informed her.

'Over me?' asked Ziza with delight.

She looked admiringly at Imre's face, stroked his hair.

'He's beautiful. I'll have him anytime.'

'No,' said Dobi. 'That he can't get you into the Castle.'

She turned slowly to face him.

'The Castle?' The thought made her shiver. 'You win the bet,' she said to Dobi, suddenly unsmiling. 'I'm not going there!'

'Why not?' asked Imre with drunken interest.

Ziza turned to him with an air of superior knowledge.

'Haven't you heard what they are saying about the Countess?'

Her voice was hard and accusing.

'She's a witch...'

'A witch!' laughed Imre delightedly.

'All the Bathorys are witches,' continued Ziza seriously.

'They sold their souls to the Devil. Their ancestor was a dragon with seven heads. And the worst of them all is the Countess Elizabeth!'

'Seven-headed dragons!' roared Imre helplessly.

With unrelenting assurance, Ziza continued, 'They say she rubs the brains of week-old babies against the door...and twists her hair on a nail bathed in blood, so she can talk to her family in seven countries.'

The absurdity of this tirade was too much for Imre, who almost fell out of his seat with laughter. As the tears streamed down the young officer's face, Dobi grabbed Ziza's arm and forced her to face him.

'Fifty kröner if you come with us!' he offered quietly.

'Fifty?'

The amount promised was five times her usual fee, yet still Ziza hesitated, so great was her fear of the Castle.

'And my protection from the witch,' urged Dobi.

She looked at Imre who had slumped drunkenly in his seat. His intoxication did not detract from his attractiveness. She turned back to Dobi.

'Promise?' she asked.

Dobi nodded and smiled reassuringly.

'Oh well, I never was one to listen to gossip,' she decided.

'Come on.'

Together they dragged the semi-conscious young officer to his feet, ignoring his protests. Then they guided him across the inn and left unnoticed - except by the clown and his companions. The circus folk cast surly looks at Dobi and whispered secretly among themselves.

In her room, the Countess knelt before a single glimmering candle, mouthing prayers to the Almighty. When the prayer was finished, and her beauty had not returned, she repeated her prayers, this time addressing her supplications to the Evil One. Her grieving countenance must have been repulsive even to Satan, because the candle flickered rapidly like a dying man's heart and went out.

Swaying, she rose to her feet.

'Dobi! Julie!' She gave vent to her hopelessness in a wail that echoed through the upper stories of the castle.

Dobi had not yet returned, Julie was visiting a relative and the sound so chilled the servants, that they crossed themselves and did not dare leave their tiny rooms.

The Countess staggered desperately to her dressing table and looked into the mirror. In the moonlight, the sight that presented itself looked so ghastly that she clasped both hands to her face, to make sure it really was hers. She had aged decades beyond her real years. Her face was hideously pitted and scarred and swollen with red carbuncles. Shrieking her fury, she snatched a perfume bottle and flung it at the mirror, shattering the hateful visage. She looked down and gasped. Her ugliness was reproduced a dozen times in the splintered shards of glass.

The Countess fell back from the merciless mirrors and staggered wildly around the room, grinding her teeth and whining like a wounded animal. The shadow of a latticed partition fell upon her like the bars of a cage, imprisoning her. She gripped the bars of the partition with shaking hands and slowly sank to the floor, bitterness tearing her down. Her anger expressed itself in strangled sobs, and then in the trembling hysteria of complete and abject despair.

Up the torchlit stairs of the tower, Dobi led Imre and Ziza, laughing and stumbling. Seeing Dobi's disapproval of their clamour, they turned and hushed each other in exaggerated whispers. This appeared so hilarious that they fell to laughing once more.

Under Dobi's expert touch the secret panel in the marble fireplace swung open and they emerged into the bedroom corridor of the castle. No one was in sight and silence reigned except for Ziza's giggling. Hastily, Dobi led them towards his room. Imre stumbled along, attempting to nuzzle Ziza's pretty, bare shoulder. She squealed at his touch. Dobi turned and, with a look, cautioned them to silence. Imre made a dumb show of sincere apology and clapped a hand over Ziza's giggling mouth. Together they entered the darkness of Dobi's room.

Dobi lit some candles and produced a bottle of strong schnapps from its hiding place. He watched approvingly as Imre collapsed onto the bed, then poured two glasses of the powerful liquor.

Ziza kicked off her shoes and began to pull off her dress. Hardly aware of his actions, Imre reached out for her, capturing a leg.

'Patience, my sweet, you'll soon get what you want,' promised Ziza, flopping him back onto the bed, where he stirred like an upturned beetle. Eagerly, she threw off her dress. Beneath it she was completely naked and her firm white body rippled invitingly in the candlelight.

Murmuring endearments, she climbed onto the bed beside Imre

and began to divest him of his trousers. Dobi stood up and placed the drinks on the bedside table, within easy reach of the lovers. Imre started to protest about something to Dobi, but the Captain merely smiled and gave Ziza a powerful slap on her heaving rump.

'Have fun, my little ones,' he grinned and strode out, locking the door behind him.

Imre vaguely remembered what he had meant to say to Dobi. He had wanted to say that Ilona would not approve and perhaps he had better get back to his own bed. Then Ziza was pressing her mouth wetly on his and her hot, naked body was squeezing against him and he forgot to say anything.

In the blackness of her room, the old Countess was almost insane. She ran from one end of the room to the other, working herself up into a dreadful fury. She talked to herself, but the sound was more like an animal snarling than human speech. As she paced, she struck out at vases and other chinaware, smashing them to pieces.

When she had broken everything there was to break, she began to slash and tear the drapes and curtains. All her evocative satins and velours, her Persian silks, were ripped to pitiful tatters. And with them her splendid memories of youth. Then she turned on her jewels. She scattered them over the floor and stamped down on her precious rings and pearls. Finally, when all her energy was used up by anger, she collapsed before the huge bed and lay writhing on the wreckage-strewn carpet. All her life was gone, forgotten. There was nothing left of Countess Elizabeth, except her burning desire to be young again. At any and most dreadful cost.

Dobi was hurrying down the corridor towards the Countess's room. He could hardly contain his anticipation. He would show the Countess how a real man made love! He would feel her quivering to her climax again and again beneath his forceful body, until she cried out that there was such a thing as too much pleasure and screamed for him to stop. And then he would show her his little surprise. And she would be his - for always.

Ahead of him, a hidden panel swung silently open and Dobi stepped quickly into the shadows. An instant later, a dark figure emerged through the gap. Dobi seized the intruder, circling his neck with crushing hands and almost lifting him off the ground. He sprung his dagger from its scabbard. The intruder cried out in terror. It was Fabio, the elderly scholar. Angrily, Dobi put him down without much gentleness.

Fabio hugged his throat and coughed uncomfortably. 'Oh gallant Captain...' he spluttered. 'I mistook you for a ghost!'

Dobi glared at the puny scholar.

'And I took you for a villain and damn near cut your throat,' he retorted, sheathing his knife with obvious disappointment.

'And what's your business here anyway?' he demanded.

Still shaken, Fabio held up a map he was carrying.

'Well, I've found a most intriguing map, which marks doors and passages I never knew existed. I've been tracing them.'

He was aware that it sounded a very lame excuse. Dobi regarded him suspiciously.

'At this hour?'

'My mind is most alert at night.' A touch of sarcasm entered his voice as he added, 'Whilst others sleep.'

The Steward poked him in the chest with a bony finger that made Fabio wince.

'Well, keep to the library,' he advised. 'Do what you like in there, but don't go prowling about. You might frighten somebody.'

'Or end up a ghost myself,' said Fabio eyeing his antagonist's dagger. Laughing nervously, he shuffled away and entered the library under Dobi's cold scrutiny. Turning, Dobi continued up the corridor. Reaching the Countess's door, he listened for a second. There was no sound from within. Smiling, he knocked quietly on the door and entered.

The room was in darkness, but he saw by the moonlight that her disturbed bed lay starkly empty. The room was a shambles, littered with broken crockery and glass. He reached for his dagger.

'Dobi?'

The weak voice made him start. It was a groan from beyond the grave. He stepped uneasily forward in the direction of the sound. Now he could see the Countess lying slumped on the floor in her nightdress. He peered into the dark, trying to make out what had happened to her.

Slowly and painfully, she crawled towards him and into the

light of the moon. He saw her face and an involuntary gasp of horror left him. Her loathsome visage - now truly hideous - was tear-stained and her transparent nightdress hung loosely upon the withered body in a pathetic mockery of her former beauty.

He stepped towards her, lip curled in disgust. As he approached, she reached out her hands towards him, pleading for help. Repulsed, he stopped, and glared down at the hag before him.

'You cheated me,' he said in quiet rage.

'No!' Again the frightful whisper.

She crawled forward and clung to his leg. He shifted his foot uncomfortably, tempted to end her piteous existence with a kick.

'You knew it would happen. You got me aroused and then made a fool of me,' he accused.

'No, I promise you,' rasped the Countess.

Dobi knelt beside her and, taking the haggard face contemptuously in his hands, he held it against his own. By simply applying pressure, he knew he could crush her skull like a mouldy marrow. Yet, he could not bring himself to do it. They had shared too much love, too many good times, although those days now seemed long gone.

'What do you want?' he asked, pronouncing each word with heavy irony that cut into her like a barb.

'That we two make love? Now? As you are? Two old fools fumbling at each other!' He laughed disdainfully and pushed her face away. She crumpled back onto the floor.

'Don't be brutal with me,' she whispered. 'Help me!'

'Why should I help you?' snapped Dobi, getting to his feet and towering over her.

'You don't want me. It's him you're thinking about. Young Imre...'

'No, it isn't true,' protested the Countess.

'And how pretty you'll look for him tomorrow. But you still need me...as a whore needs her pander.'

The Countess began to weep again. He looked down at her dispassionately. Perhaps she had suffered enough, but his pleasure had been denied him and for that she would pay dearly. Now was the time to spring his surprise, he decided.

'Well, there's one customer who doesn't want you any more, young or old,' he taunted.

She looked up uncomprehendingly.

'Your lover...' he smiled, smug in his secret knowledge.

'What are you talking about?' asked the Countess, her voice stronger now, as her willpower responded to Dobi's jibes.

He chuckled and, leaning down, dragged her to her feet.

He snatched a shawl from a nearby chair and threw it around her scrawny body.

'I'll show you,' replied Dobi, savouring his cruel game. 'Come and watch him get satisfaction from a real young woman...'

'No,' said the Countess, denying the possibility.

'Yes! At this very moment he is lying on my bed, coupling with the cheapest whore in town! Enjoying what you can never give him again!'

He pulled her, resisting, to the door and out into the corridor. She blinked at the sudden light of the flambeaux lining the walls. Dobi let go of her wrist and smiled challengingly, daring her to come and test the truth of his claim. Turning on his heel, he strode off down the corridor. After a moment's indecision, she followed. Together they hurried along the passage, the tall, upright soldier, and the bent, frail old woman scurrying to keep up his pace.

The Countess's heart beat fiercely and her stomach churned as they approached the door to Dobi's room. She had lost her youth and now it appeared she had lost her lover. If Imre really had forsaken the beauty of her other self for the sweaty embraces of a strumpet, there was no reason left for her to live. She might as well cast her decaying body off the top of the battlements and bring her misery to its end.

Dobi halted before his door and produced a key. The Countess watched grimly as he turned the key in the lock and swung the door quietly open for her, with a conjurer's flourish.

The room was well-lit by candles and she had no difficulty seeing the bed. On it lay Imre apparently asleep. As she looked in, he stirred and rolled over.

On the bed beside him sat a plump heavy-lidded whore, whose face carried too much make-up. She was dressing with brisk movements and the Countess caught sight of her white breasts hanging like over-ripe fruit, before she fastened her dress. Tears welled up in the Countess's eyes. She had been betrayed. Once the toast of the noblest court in Christendom, she had been passed over for a cheap whore.

Imre stirred restlessly, and fearing he would waken and see her, the Countess stepped back into the shadows of the corridor. Ziza looked up at the movement and saw Dobi framed in the doorway. With an angry cry, she jumped up and advanced towards him, hands defiantly on hips. Her pride had evidently been hurt.

'What's your game, eh? Pushing me onto a little bastard who doesn't want me!'

Dobi glared at her, willing her to hold her tongue before his intrigue was revealed to the Countess. Ziza was vaguely aware of a red-eyed old woman standing in the corridor, but in her anger, she took no notice.

'What's the matter?' she cried, grabbing hold of Dobi's arm and shaking it. 'Can't he do it or something? You ought to give him a few lessons!'

She turned to look back disgustedly at Imre, who still lay fast asleep.

'A whole night's work wasted and I want my money!'

'Shut up and wait in there,' growled Dobi. The angry whore tried to push past him, but he flung her back in the room and locked the door in her face. He ignored the angry pounding that immediately started up. Slowly, he turned to the Countess. When he saw her face with its hate-filled eyes, he knew she had understood everything.

'I see what you did,' she said accusingly. 'You made him drunk.'

'No I didn't,' protested Dobi striving to look indignant.

The Countess seemed to have regained her composure. The self-pitying look was gone, replaced by her more usual expression of hardness and authority. She stood upright again, once more mistress of the castle.

'Be quiet,' she said sharply. 'So you brought the slut here, did you?'

She nodded approvingly, a thin cruel smile appearing as a plan formed in her mind.

'Good, how very thoughtful of you, Dobi. Imre doesn't need her, but I do.' Her voice became a command. 'Bring her to me. Now!'

Without waiting to hear his protests, she turned and walked

purposefully back to her room. Dismayed, Dobi watched her. He knew he was defeated. He had prepared an ingenious trap, and he was the only one to fall into it. A black look on his face, he unlocked his door again and stepped inside. Ziza jumped up angrily from the bed as he entered.

'Where's my money then?' she demanded. 'Where is it? It's not my fault the bastard's asleep,' she said with a disdainful flick of the head towards the sleeping youth. 'I want my fifty kröner!'

Ignoring her, Dobi walked to the bed and examined Imre, turning him onto his back. His breathing was deep and rhythmic. There was no point in waking him, decided Dobi. He had passed out and would be unconscious until morning at least. The sleep of the dead. Dobi smiled sardonically. Behind him Ziza stepped up, her voice shrewish with anger at his refusal to acknowledge her.

'Did you hear me?' She clutched his arm. 'I want my money!'

'All right, all right.' Dobi's voice was suddenly friendly, his manner conciliatory. He opened the money pouch hanging from his belt and presented her with ten heavy coins. Open-mouthed, she stared at them.

'A hundred kröner?' she asked incredulously.

Dobi nodded. 'For a better client. You had no fun here? Well, you'll have some now,' he promised suavely.

Ziza did not yet look convinced of his good intentions, so he hastily added:

'It's not a man, it's a woman. She sometimes has peculiar tastes. She might want...' he paused heavily, 'some special favours.'

He made it sound a very interesting experience.

Ziza giggled happily, her breeziness returning.

'For a hundred, I'd take on the whole Turkish harem,' she said enthusiastically.

'Here, it's not the Witch, is it?' she asked with sudden apprehension.

Dobi laughed at her fear.

'I thought you knew,' he said, 'she only takes her pleasure with the Devil.'

Ziza nodded seriously, accepting his words as gospel.

Dobi softly blew out the candles and guided Ziza into the corridor. In the doorway he paused to look at Imre. The soldier was still sound asleep. Dobi closed the door and hastened Ziza along the corridor towards the Countess's room. Ziza's bawdy laughter sounded nervous as it rippled like an intruder along the bleak stone walls of the corridor.

From behind a crack in the library door, Fabio watched them go. He was breathless with excitement. From his hiding place he had witnessed everything - the drunken arrival of Imre and the whore, the Countess's anger and her strange subsequent interest in the prostitute. Quietly, Fabio closed the door and turned back into the library.

He had known that something mysterious was taking place in the castle, something that concerned the Countess and her mysterious disappearances. Now Fabio thought he knew what the secret was. It was horrifying, unbelievable, but it made sense.

He moved briskly to the bookshelf he had seen Dobi consult a few nights previously. Soon his weak eyes spied the volume that the Steward had taken such an interest in. Gingerly, he pulled the old book down, feeling an uncomfortable sensation at the contact with the strange leather binding. He vaguely wondered what animal had provided the skin for the unusual binding - a curious pink, soft and warm to the touch.

Bearing the book triumphantly to the desk, he laid it down and pulled up a chair. He began to turn the big vellum pages with an unsteady hand. The strange symbols and characters that decorated some of the pages left him aghast. He knew the meanings of only a few but that was sufficient for him to know that the book possessed a terrible and fantastic knowledge.

He quickly thumbed through the yellowed ageing pages until he came to a section at the back penned in a different hand, more recent in origin. The title of the chapter was "Blood Sacrifices". Spellbound, he began to read.

When he finally shut the book, Fabio was trembling and his face was as white as his beard. There was no longer any doubt in his mind that he had uncovered the Countess's dreadful secret.

To the Countess the idea was probably new, but Fabio had come across the concept, in more theoretical terms, many times in his studies. 'For the blood is the life' said the Bible. Was it not, after all, the foundation of life in all creatures?

A man grows from a babe and becomes an old man and dies.

Throughout that time he goes through many changes, in thought and appearance, but the flow of blood in his veins is constant until his death. Was it not true then, mused Fabio, that man's blood contained the sum of his experiences and perhaps more. Maybe it also contained his qualities, even his very personality. Could not those qualities be passed on to another through the absorption of his blood? After all, the wise Romans had drunk the warm blood of dying gladiators to gain their strength and hardiness. And Pope Sextus V had bathed in the blood of oxen, believing it to be a purifying tonic.

The chapter on Blood Sacrifices had been full of spells and incantations, much of it nonsense to be sure, thought Fabio. Yet the basis was firm. Many alchemists had come to the conclusion that blood, the primordial substance, was the answer to the age-old search for the Philosopher's Stone. This legendary device had been sought for in everything from the innards of toads to the milk of women. Perhaps the answer had been pumping through the veins of the despairing seekers all along.

The importance of the Philosopher's Stone was in its powers of transmutation. It was said to be able to change coal into diamonds, glass into gold, and to make the corrupt whole again. Fabio's old friend, Paracelsus, the master alchemist himself, was believed to have experimented with the transmuting potential of blood, trying to transform children into grown men and giving youth back to the old. Rumours had spoken of his success but this had never been substantiated.

It seemed that Countess Elizabeth had stumbled upon the same discovery, her motives being rather more selfish than those of idealistic Paracelsus. Fabio remembered that Italian noblewomen were said to preserve their complexions by rubbing the blood of doves gently into their offending wrinkles. It seemed that the Countess's method was more demanding but also, if his suspicions were correct, more effective. The blood of the murdered girls must impart the whole of their youthful vitality and beauty to the ageing Countess.

One thing puzzled Fabio. Now that he had uncovered the Countess's secret, what was he to do about it?

Denounce her to the bailiffs? And would they believe him if he tried?

**When Ziza stepped into the Countess's room, urged
on by Dobi's prodding hand, she had found it in
darkness. By the glow of the moon she could see
the huge bed, with its dragon-teeth crest above the pillow,
was empty. Behind her, the door closed and she knew a
moment's panic. The heavy coins in her purse reassured her
and she stepped forward into the room.**

It was in a dreadful shambles with bits of torn cloth and broken
pots everywhere underfoot. They must have had a proper orgy in
here, thought Ziza excitedly. They certainly knew how to enjoy
themselves, these aristocrats. Ziza fervently hoped that she might
soon latch on to a doddery old Baron, or, better, a dashing Count
who would whisk her away to his castle and set her up as the
lady of the manor.

'Come nearer. You're not shy I hope!'

Ziza jumped at the unexpected voice. So there was someone
in the room after all. It had been a woman's voice, hard and
used to giving orders, but not unfriendly. Suppressing a giggle, Ziza stepped into the moonlight, showing herself off to
the hidden watcher. She peered into the darkness, but still
could not see the other person.

'You have a lovely body,' said the voice. 'You shouldn't hide it
with those clothes.'

The voice came from somewhere over in the corner furthest
from her. Ziza smiled. This was a bashful customer but she had a
pleasant way of putting things.

Ziza stripped off her dress with the casual ease of someone
who has spent a lifetime undressing, professionally and otherwise. Soon she stood naked and very pale in the moonlight. She
tried not to shiver but it was chilly in the dark room. She arched
her body, letting her unseen admirer see her well-known attribut-
es at their best.

'Exquisite, my dear.'

The voice was nearer now and Ziza stared apprehensively
across the room. Out of the dark shadows stepped a woman
dressed in a long black dress with a high white ruff. Her face was
still hidden but Ziza guessed her to be in late middle age. She
remembered the old woman she had glimpsed in the corridor
with Dobi. It could not be the same person. That had been a real-

ly haggard old woman. This person stood erect, had an air of authority.

Ziza would have preferred a younger admirer, but she did not really mind. She enjoyed the caresses of women. They seemed gentle and sincere. Not at all like the greasy clutches of beer-breathed men.

'So you expected to be making love to Lieutenant Imre?' asked the woman in the black dress. That snotty bastard, thought Ziza; she was well rid of him.

'Yes, milady. But I'm glad to be here instead.'

'So am I.'

Ziza could sense her smiling across the darkness.

'Come here, I want to kiss you.'

Smiling invitingly, Ziza lifted her head and took a step towards the waiting woman.

She did not see the flash of the knife in the moonlight as it swished down towards her. Her attention was riveted to the woman's ugly, hate-filled face and when she saw those lustrous eyes, glaring madly in the dark, she knew, without doubt, that this was her, the Devil Woman, the Witch!

Then the blade slashed across her throat and all she knew was blood and death.

When Dobi heard Ziza's agonised cry, he stepped into the room. The Countess was bending over the body, slashing the whore's wrists. She did it without feeling or thought, as if she were butchering a calf. Dobi sighed. No more tempestuous Saturday nights with Ziza...

'Don't just stand there! We're losing precious blood,' bemoaned the Countess. Quickly, Dobi lit some candles and went to the Countess's aid. He lifted the lifeless body on to the huge silver bowl the Countess had prepared. The blood from the severed throat and wrists jetted darkly into the bowl, quickly filling it.

Ziza's eyes were wide open, like those of a cow hanging in a slaughter-house. They stared reproachfully at Dobi. Gently, he leaned down and closed them.

On a shelf, he found an unbroken bottle of wine and a glass. He slumped wearily into an armchair and poured himself a glass. He looked and felt older than usual. The rich liquid in his glass looked distastefully red to him, but he gulped it down and its searing heat along his throat felt good.

In the bathroom, the old Countess put the bowl of thick arterial blood down on her dressing table. She seated herself before the mirror and dipped a large sponge into the blood.

With quick, dextrous strokes, she applied the blood to her face, the sponge leaving large red smears across her cheeks and forehead. The blood began to cake dry. The Countess put down the sponge and, using a damp towel, started to wash the congealed blood from her face.

When this was done, she flicked the towel aside and turned expectantly back to the mirror. Icy fear gripped her as she saw her reflection. The miraculous change had not taken place. Her face remained as worn and shrivelled as before.

Dobi jumped to his feet in surprise as the Countess stumbled into the room, panic showing in her face.

'Look at me!' she cried. 'I did the same as before but there's no change. What went wrong?'

He stared at her, wondering what could have prevented the transformation. They must have omitted some part of the ritual. But what? He frowned, and then he remembered the book. The Book of Mysteries. It would hold the answer. He hurried towards the door.

'Where are you going?'

He paused in the doorway.

'To get the book.'

'What book?' asked the Countess, anxious to hear of any method that would free her from her prison of ugliness.

'Wait here,' instructed Dobi and hastened from the room.

His footsteps echoing noisily along the corridor, Dobi made for the library. He pushed the door open and entered its musty gloom. A candle still burned weakly and he made straight for the shelf where the book was kept.

It was not where he had left it. Anxiously he scoured the neighbouring shelves, then angrily began throwing books to the floor.

'Is this what you're looking for?'

Fabio's taunt made him whirl round. The old man was standing in the shadows, his spectacles showing fluttering images of the candle before him. In his upraised right hand, he held the open book.

With a furious cry, Dobi whipped out his dagger and made for the old man, vaulting over a chair in his eagerness to cut the scholar's throat. Fabio bleated with fright but moved surprisingly fast. He ripped the important chapter from the book and held the pages over the candle in a trembling hand.

Across the table between them, Dobi lunged with his dagger. Fabio snatched the candle and moved quickly to another corner of the table. He was careful to hold the quivering pages above the candle flame. Looking up, he saw Dobi preparing to leap onto the table, his face intent on cruelty.

'If you kill me, gallant Captain,' Fabio cried shrilly, 'Your mistress will never know the truth!'

Gripping his dagger tightly, Dobi hesitated. The room was silent except for their heavy breathing as they faced each other, separated by only a few feet of wood. Grinning, Dobi began to work around the table, determined to finally rid himself of the verbose nuisance.

The Countess's voice rang out curtly. 'Leave him,' she commanded.

They turned to see her standing in the doorway, her eyes fixed fiercely on Dobi.

'Don't trust him,' protested Dobi. The idea of Fabio's continued existence seemed to pain him.

'Trust me and I will help you,' cried Fabio quickly. His breathing was coming in spluttering gasps and he was almost laughing with fear as he appealed to the old woman.

'Choose, Countess!'

Dobi glared murderously at the scholar, then slowly backed away. He gestured for Fabio to read the pages held in his shaking hand.

Nervously, Fabio held a page up to the wan light. 'The chapter on Blood Sacrifices...' he began.

Dobi's reaction was quick and contemptuous.

'Yes, yes, I've read it!'

'But not quite far enough, Captain,' snapped back Fabio. 'Or else you wouldn't have made such a stupid mistake!'

Dobi and the Countess waited, eager to share his knowledge.

Fabio consulted one of the pages.

'It states quite clearly...' He began to read: '"For the restoration of youth and beauty... only the blood of a Virgin may be used."'

The Countess cut into his narrative.

'She was a common whore,' she said with realisation.

Fabio bowed to her, congratulating her on her keen perception.

'Ah, well, there you are...' he said condescendingly.

The Countess turned angrily on Dobi.

'You fool! Have you no sense?'

Dobi said nothing but turned resentfully from her gaze.

The Countess faced Fabio from behind a taut smile.

'Thank you' Master Fabio, for your scholarship on the matter. It will not go unrewarded.' There was the barest hint of a threat in the last words. Fabio sensed it and it made him smile nervously.

'Countess, if I can assist you at any time,' he offered hastily. 'I find the whole subject most enthralling and would be pleased to help.'

The Countess smiled graciously in appreciation of his offer. When she turned to Dobi, her face was hard once more.

'Come, Dobi,' she summoned. 'Tomorrow you will make good your mistake.'

She swept majestically from the room.

Before following her, Dobi turned and glared at Fabio. 'Remember, Captain, a virgin,' jibed the old man. Dobi turned coldly and stalked out.

Outside the library, the Countess waited as Dobi slammed the door behind him. He joined her, shaking his head.

'You're mad to trust him,' he said.

'Why?' The Countess challenged him with a look of self-assurance. 'Let him live in fear of his life. That way, he will never betray us.' Together, they walked in silence back to the Countess's room.

Behind the door of the library, Fabio sighed with relief as he heard their departing footsteps. He had been expecting Dobi to rush back in and stick him like a pig with his dagger or sword. Weeping softly, he sank to the floor, almost fainting from the nervous exhaustion of terror.

It was market day in Veres and the main square was a scene of riotous confusion. Dealers noisily contested each other in declaiming the excellence of their goods - from fresh vegetables to rough earthenware pottery, coarse cloth and sturdy, hand-stitched leather clothes. Their voices competed with the scarcely more vacuous cries of the main attraction, the livestock. There were goats, sheep, cackling geese, chickens, horses and cows and each contributed their particular vocal personality to the cacophony as they came under the keen-eyed scrutiny of visiting farmers and landowners.

Through the melée children gambolled and chased each other, upsetting the poultry-seller who found himself chasing his stock after every fast-footed passing of the urchins.

Mixing with the buyers and dealers were the idle and the curious and the simple poor. And the itinerant peddlers, each preceded by his special call - the pie-man, the hot potato seller, the colourful tinker and the egg-man. There were beggars, hucksters, purveyors of custard flans, vagabonds and a knife-grinder working his treadle and showering passers-by with sparks.

Today, the scene was made still more colourful by the intrusion of strange new sights rubbing shoulders with the gawking crowd - a bearded lady, blackamoors, tumblers, midgets, a strong man and the sharp-faced Fool spreading laughter.

Through this motley throng moved the Steward of the castle, looking aloof and purposeful. In his black-gloved hand twitched a riding crop and those who saw him coming were quick to avoid his path. Tradesmen implored him in vain to inspect their goods. He had no evident wish to fondle pigs or cows. He was after livestock of a different kind.

Behind the pens for cattle and other animals, stood a group of similar stalls. Except here the trade was in human beings. A squire could buy himself a new servant to replace one he had recently beaten to death, and peasants sold unwanted or mischievous children and were pleased to be rid of an extra hungry mouth. Most of the bargains to be procured were children, but there was one stall displaying females of various ages. It was to here that Dobi directed his steps.

Inspecting the wares, he quickly dismissed the older women as being of no interest to him. There were several pert, straw-haired girls of thirteen or fourteen but their faces were too pretty for them to have remained virgins, he decided.

The Seller, a scraggy, fast-talking peasant, noted Dobi's curiosity and pointed his stick towards a buxom country lass with a heavy bovine face.

'Look at this one, sir,' he exhorted. 'Feel the muscles in those arms. And these thighs, they can pull the weight of a carriage!'

Demonstrating, he lifted her arms and pinched her muscles and thighs in a similar way to the nearby cattle-dealers. Seeing the eyes of the proud, greying soldier were on her, the girl pulled herself upright, emphasising her firm, jutting breasts, as she had been told.

'Breasts of solid teak! A pleasure to feel, sir,' cried the Seller, slipping the girl's blouse off her shoulder and cupping the black-nippled breast. Dobi ignored the peasant's invitation to feel these wonders for himself.

'She can work longer hours than anyone I know. A bargain for a hundred kröner,' urged the salesman.

He forced her head down in Dobi's direction, a lascivious, rotten-toothed grin on his face. 'And I tell you, she's willing as well...'

Wordlessly, Dobi moved on, his attention caught by a young figure slumped piteously in the mud beside the stall. The girl was about fifteen, skinny and fair with protruding teeth and lustreless eyes that proclaimed her an idiot. Her clothes were soiled and, as Dobi watched, her head lolled aimlessly from side to side.

'How much for this one?' he queried.

'What?' exclaimed the Seller in disbelief.

'This one here,' said Dobi, stepping over to the girl and prodding her with his riding crop. He used it to lift her skirt and glanced at her pale, thin thighs. The Seller came and stood beside him, bemused by his interest in the girl.

'Young Bertha? She's one of my own.'

He stared down at the girl appraisingly.

'Well, you can take her off my hands for free...if you take a goat for twenty-five,' he added hastily.

'Has she ever been with a man?' asked Dobi, trying to sound disinterested.

The Seller roared with mirth.

'Are you joking?'

Bending down, he stuck a horny thumb in the girl's mouth and yanked back her lips, revealing Bertha's crooked protruding teeth more fully.

'Can you imagine anyone who would want to?' guffawed the peasant.

'I'll take her,' said Dobi flatly, reaching into his pouch for the required amount. Chuckling, the Seller tied a length of rope round a lean goat's neck and offered the other end to the Steward. Dobi hesitated, then, with a slight grimace, he accepted the rope and the goat and handed over the money. They turned to Bertha.

Slowly, the girl got to her feet, wrapped a red shawl around her shoulders and picked up her pathetic bundle of belongings. She gave her father a last laconic hug and trudged defeatedly after her new master.

With Bertha at his heels, Dobi strode through the bustling crowd, leading the goat in an aristocratic manner worthy of a mastiff. He passed right by the circus wagon where the three remaining gypsy girls were entertaining a crowd with their dancing - but he paid them no heed. Nor was he aware of the cunning eyes of the clown watching him as he made his way back to the castle with his purchases.

In Dobi's room, Imre gave voice to a low groan as he rose from the bed and a throbbing pain pounded at his temples. He had little memory of the previous night except that he remembered he had visited the Shepherd's Inn and spoken with Captain Balogh. What transpired subsequently was a mystery save for one point: he had obviously had too much to drink. He imagined Dobi resentfully carrying his unconscious body back from the Inn and he smiled, until the pain shot through his skull and he clapped his hands to his head and groaned.

Experimentally, he tried a few uneasy steps and managed to reach a wash-bowl of cold water. He plunged his head into its shocking coolness. When he raised his streaming face, he was feeling improved and refreshed, except that there remained a taste of stables in his mouth.

He shook his head, and the floating vagueness in his mind sprang into sharper focus. Remembering he had not seen Ilona the previous evening, he decided he could not wait another minute without paying her a visit.

The corridor was empty when Imre emerged from Dobi's room. His feet remembering how to walk, Imre made his way towards Ilona's room.

Outside her door, he hesitated, realising he had no idea of time. It might be five in the morning for all he knew. Casting his doubts aside, he knocked and entered.

Countess Elizabeth looked up sharply as he walked in. They were both startled to see each other, Imre more so. He did not remember the Countess looking quite that ugly and old. He attributed this to the illness that had kept her confined to her room.

She was staring at him with her bright grey eyes that were so similar to Ilona's. She seemed unable to speak so Imre broke the awkward silence.

'Countess, I'm sorry to disturb you. I'm looking for your daughter.'

The old Countess smiled back at him and, despite her ugliness and the apparent ravages of her illness, her smile was sweet.

'She went out early - to gather some flowers,' said the Countess easily. Imre noticed that she was occupied with laying out some gowns, colourful and sumptuous in contrast to her own gloomy black garment. He assumed they belonged to Ilona.

'Please forgive my intrusion,' said Imre and turned to go.

The Countess held up a shrivelled hand.

'Wait! Please stay. We have much to talk about, I think.'

'Yes,' replied Imre, judging from the warmth of her voice that she was referring to him and Ilona.

The Countess laid the gorgeous green satin robe she was holding down on the bed and gestured for him to sit in a chair. When he had seated himself, she came and sat opposite. There was a strained silence as Imre struggled to gather his thoughts.

The Countess picked up a silver goblet of pink sugared almonds and offered them. He refused politely. The chewing would play havoc with his slowly surfacing mind. He wished he had had time to rehearse the scene they were now playing.

'I wanted to speak to you before, but Ilona told me of your illness. I'm very happy to see you better and moving about.'

The Countess acknowledged his sympathy with a gracious nod and a quick smile.

'I'm a little better today,' she admitted. 'But I'm not at all well. The shock of these last few days, you understand.'

'Of course.' Imre smiled compassionately. Then he took a deep breath and plunged into the speech his brain was trying hard to compose.

'Ilona will have told you -'

'That you are in love and wish to be married,' cut in the Countess helpfully.

'I sincerely hope you approve,' said Imre, nodding.

There was a brief pause during which Imre waited with bated breath. Then, the Countess smiled and Imre knew that there was to be no opposition to his marriage.

'It was always the wish of my dear late husband that you, the son of his dearest friend, should one day meet our daughter.'

The Countess punctuated her reminiscence with a regretful sigh.

'Alas, he did not live to see it.'

She stared tragically at the sugared almonds for a moment. When she lifted her face, she was smiling and there were droplets forming in her grey eyes.

'But you have made his widow very happy, Lieutenant.'

Imre's relief and gratitude were enormous, much more than he could express in words. Moved by the Countess's words, he said with passionate sincerity, 'Believe me, Countess... I shall honour and cherish Ilona for the rest of my days.'

The Countess regarded him affectionately and motioned for him to sit at her feet.

'Come kneel beside me.'

Obediently, Imre sprang from his chair and knelt beside her, taking her thick-veined hand in his and kissing it devoutly. With her other hand, the Countess gently stroked his wild brown hair, and lowered his face slowly into her lap. He lay there without speaking, unashamed of the tears of gratitude in his own eyes. The Countess continued to caress him with a motherly hand.

'My son,' she softly murmured. 'My son.'

After a moment, she became restlessly aroused, and had greater difficulty in keeping her caresses motherly. Furiously, she began to hope that Dobi had procured a virgin for her bloodbath.

It was a warm day and a fine yellow haze lay upon the forest.

Janco was lumbering towards the hut, laden with a heap of faggots for the fire. Juggling his load in one arm, he took the key from his belt with the other and unlocked the door. It swung open, revealing the gloomy oppression of the ill-lit interior. He stepped inside.

Still clutching his load, he locked the door behind him. Turning, he glanced over towards his captive and immediately dropped his sticks. They tumbled noisily to the floor.

Ilona was lying stretched out on the heap of dirty sacking that served as her bed. Her skirt rose high on her thigh and her frilly blouse was undone, revealing her young woman's breasts. A pink rosebud of a nipple seemed to wink invitingly at Janco. Her brown hair had been let down and curled over one shoulder. Her lips pouted suggestively and her blue eyes were warm and encouraging...

Janco's eyes threatened to fall out of his head. He gurgled with desire and moved, slobbering, towards her. As he loomed above her, Ilona steeled herself to receive his attentions.

Slowly, he reached out and touched her hair. She smiled all the more invitingly. Reassured, he took her face in his filthy hand and began to caress her cheek with a coarse gentleness. Grunting lustful, senseless endearments, he lowered his bulk on to her, pressing her into the bed of sacking. His grimy hand plucked her breast and began to fondle it as he brought his tongueless mouth down on hers.

Ilona screwed her eyes shut and stifled a cry of revulsion. It was a necessary ordeal. Her own hands were as busy as the mute's and had already located the key to freedom hanging on his belt. Carefully, she managed to unhook the key without disturbing his ardour.

She looked at her would-be lover, inches away from her own face. His eyes were closed in ecstasy as he rubbed himself against her and fumbled at his clothes.

Gripping the key tightly in her fist, Ilona suddenly slid out from under the groping mute and ran quickly to the door and forced the shaking key into the lock. Surprised and angry, Janco clambered to his feet and lurched after her, arms outstretched.

Desperately, Ilona struggled to turn the key in the lock. Janco bore down on her, clucking angrily. Turning, she pushed against a nearby table and sent it skidding across the floor into the oncoming figure. It knocked him against the wall, momentarily winding him.

Which was all the time Ilona needed. The key turned in the lock and, a second later, she escaped through the door and out into the welcoming sunlight. Shaking his head to clear it, Janco struggled up and followed.

Ilona ran from the hut as fast as she could. It was hard going. She had been cramped into the hut for days and her legs felt weak and unsteady. And her dainty shoes were built for appearance, not running through a muddy forest.

Breathless and sobbing with fear, Ilona ran under the trees. Grimly, Janco followed, gaining on her at a steady pace. Tears ran down Ilona's cheeks as she realised there was little hope of outrunning her jailer.

Suddenly she slipped in the mud and hurtled into a large puddle with a resounding smack. She reappeared on the surface, completely covered in thick slimy mud. Janco ran up and watched her helpless, spluttering fury. The sight goaded him into a fit of boisterous, stomach-clutching laughter. Ilona wept.

Still laughing, Janco dragged her free of the mud and pushed her reproachfully back towards the hut. She stumbled along, clawing the mud from her eyes with short angry movements.

He shepherded her into the dismal hut and a moment later came the sharp retort of the key turning in the lock.

Imre left the Countess full of enthusiasm for the future. She had been so understanding that he was quite taken aback. Before, he had considered her harsh, cruel even. Now, with his greater knowledge of her, he realised she was a warm person with the well-being of her subjects at heart.

Such were his thoughts when a discreet hissing from nearby attracted his attention. He saw Fabio had ventured his head out of the library door and was making frantic signals. Amused by the old man's antics, Imre strolled over.

'Fabio, old man...What's the matter?' he enquired in such a loud voice that Fabio groaned and, putting his fingers to his lips, hushed him to silence.

'I have to speak to you urgently,' said Fabio. 'Have you seen the Countess Ilona today?'

'No, I'm just going to look for her,' replied Imre.

Fabio nodded grimly.

'Well, don't be surprised if you can't find her,' he counselled.

'What?'

Imre was both shocked and frightened by the scholar's words. They had not been delivered as a warning but with a sarcasm that Imre found offensive. It seemed the old man was casting some aspersion on his beloved's reliability. Imre was anxious to learn further.

Fabio was about to reveal more when he caught sight of Dobi standing outside his room, watching them intently. He immediately began to tremble in a way that was impossible for Imre not to notice.

'What's the matter?' he asked, alarmed, moving to assist the old man. Fabio pushed him away fiercely.

'I can't talk now!'

He lowered his voice and added mysteriously, 'By the stables. Tonight after supper. Wait for me!'

So saying, he slipped back into the library. Imre attempted to follow but the door was closed firmly in his face. Disconcerted, he looked round. Dobi was nowhere in sight. Slowly, Imre walked along the corridor towards the main staircase. Much of his earlier happiness seemed to have evaporated. He felt cold and disturbed and, worst of all, he did not know why.

It was night and chill, and in the Countess's bedchamber a cheery fire blazed.

Julie approached the fireplace with her usual sphinx-like smile. Methodically she began to feed some old clothes into the fire. The flames leapt up, devouring them hungrily.

They were not any of the Countess's old clothes. No furs or satin or velvet. No grand gowns beaded with pearls or topped with a lace ruff. Just poor, soiled rags that had belonged to a girl called Bertha, when she was alive.

Julie poked the ashes, watching them fall and settle. Then, she threw in the last item, Bertha's red shawl. It lay smouldering on top of the coals, smoke spiralling furiously. Then it burst into flames and was soon reduced to black, dancing ash, light as air.

Behind Julie stood Countess Elizabeth. Her lustrous eyes sparkled as she watched the flames consume Bertha's memory. As if a premonition of hellfire had been conjured in her pupils.

She turned away and stripped off her black dress, preparing her scrawny, flaccid body for the application of virgin's blood which would transform it into unearthly beauty.

In the darkness of the stable yard, Imre waited impatiently. It was unlike Fabio to be late, he thought, hunching his shoulders against the cold wind, and blowing warm breath on his chilled fingers.

Despite the early hour, there was little activity in the castle. An occasional window in the black shape of the tower reflected light, but a gloomy silence prevailed. Except for the nervous shuffling of the horses in their stalls.

Anxiously, Imre began to pace the yard. The movement helped to warm his blood. After several minutes, he stopped. There was still no sign of the old man. Imre looked up at the tower. The library was in darkness.

Abruptly, he heard a noise and turned, relief in his face.

'Fabio?' he whispered, staring into the darkness and trying to detect the scholar's shuffling figure. There was no answer. No one stepped forward. There was only the sound of hooves clicking against the ground. Imre frowned. He was anxious to hear what more the old man had to say. His prophecy about Ilona had proved entirely true. All afternoon, Imre had searched for her around the castle and in the woods, but there had been no sign. His questions had been rebuffed by lame excuses. Could something have happened to her? Something which only Fabio was willing to reveal to him. Had she been packed off to Vienna to spoil his marriage plans?

Imre made a quick decision. He would wait no longer, but go and find Fabio without delay. He strode quickly towards the looming tower and entered. He hurried up the winding stone steps two at a time. The torches, agitated by the shivery wind, cast fantastic shapes around him.

Reaching the top of the stairs, Imre pushed on the loose stone that Ilona had shown him and the secret panel swung open before him. He was in the main corridor. Closing the panel behind him, Imre crept along the corridor towards the library. As he passed the old Countess's door, he heard the sound of splashing within. Evidently the Countess was enjoying a bath. He paused outside Ilona's door, hoping to find her in. There was no sound and no light visible under the door. It seemed to prove that something had definitely happened to his fiancée. He hurried on towards the library.

Imre opened the door of the library. It was in darkness, except for a shaft of moonlight from one of the small ornate windows.

'Fabio?' whispered Imre. There was no reply and, disappointed, he turned to leave. Then he recalled that Fabio was sometimes in the habit of falling asleep over some dreary manuscript. He might well have done so and not been conscious of the passing of time. He edged forward.

The musty smell of decayed paper was strong and oppressive. As he felt his way towards Fabio's desk, the vague shapes of the bookshelves seemed massive in the murky light. Imre felt stifled and longed to leave the room and breathe fresh air. He almost stumbled over the desk. Regaining his balance, he probed the surface of the desk and found a small candle. With a spark from his tinder box he lit it. The flame was dim and cast only a feeble yellow glow. Imre stood up and strained his eyes around the jaundiced room. It seemed empty. There was nothing but books, like rows and rows of decaying teeth.

He thought he saw a movement between some distant shelves, where his light scarcely penetrated. Apprehensively, he moved towards the spot, shielding the weak flame with his hand. The dusty shelves crawled by, each harbouring a hidden assailant in Imre's imagination.

He almost walked into the feet before he saw them. They were hanging from above, on a level with his face. Wide-eyed, Imre held his candle higher in an unsteady hand.

The hanging body's head slowly revolved to greet him. Imre shrank back in horror. It was Fabio. His eyes stared sightlessly down out of his blackened face. His little round spectacles had slipped awkwardly and rested on his nose, giving him the appearance of a foolish schoolmaster. His tongue bulged from his mouth and a trickle of blood oozed from a nostril.

'Too much knowledge is a dangerous thing,' said a harsh voice behind Imre.

Imre spun round fearfully as Dobi stepped into the dancing shadows. The Steward regarded the swinging body with a melancholy smile.

'Poor man...brilliant scholar...He'd read all those books...knew everything...but now...?'

Dobi turned to Imre, shaking his head reflectively.

'He knows nothing!'

Imre was speechless with horror as he stared up at Fabio's pathetic, slowly-turning body. Casually, Dobi walked over to a table and lit an oil-lamp. The room was instantly flooded with deeper, more menacing shadows.

Throwing off his fear, Imre rounded accusingly on the Steward. 'You killed him!'

Without denying it, Dobi stared back at him with a faintly defiant smile.

'You killed him, because he knew something about you and the Countess.' Imre's voice rose angrily. 'He was going to tell me but you stopped him!'

He flung himself forward to seize Dobi. The older man was quicker and stronger. With a sudden violent movement, he hauled Imre round and pinned him against a bookcase, one powerful hand gripping his throat. Books fell and smacked to the floor about them.

'Now listen to me, you young whelp,' said Dobi, teeth clenched in anger. 'You came here, you took the stables...'

Imre fought for breath as Dobi's hand tightened, digging into his throat.

'...All right, you keep them, but the Countess is all mine, you understand, all mine...I've waited twenty years...'

Breathless, Imre stared at him, uncomprehending. Dobi released his throat, shoving him back against the shelf with contempt. Imre clutched the back of his head.

'Take her then,' he said. 'I don't want her. It's Ilona I love.'

'Ilona!' scoffed Dobi.

'Yes. Where is she? What have you done with her?'

Dobi sneered at him.

'You want to see her, you really want to see your bride?'

'Yes!' Alarmed by Dobi's jibes, Imre was beside himself with fear for Ilona's safety.

Dobi laughed knowingly. 'And so you shall. In all her glory!'

Chuckling, he made for the door.

'Follow me.'

Imre hurried after him.

Dobi strode straight for the Countess's bedchamber. Without knocking, he threw open the door and waved Imre inside, with a sarcastic bow. Hesitantly, Imre entered the Countess's forbidding chamber and looked around. It appeared to be empty, although there were broken decorations and other signs of recent violence. Not seeing Ilona, he turned questioningly to Dobi. At that moment, a voice rang out.

'Julie, is that you?'

It was Ilona's voice, but there was a harshness in it that Imre had not heard before.

The words had come from behind a screen. Dobi stepped up to it and flung it aside. It crashed to the floor with a shattering reverberation.

Imre cried out in revulsion at what lay behind the screen. Revealed to them was Ilona, standing completely naked, a look of surprise distorting her lovely face. In one hand she held a gory sponge and her whole body was smeared and dripping with blood. Beside her stood a large vessel, filled to the brim with the thick red liquid.

When she saw Imre in the room, staring at her blood-stained body, the Countess screamed and seized a towel. Before she could entirely cover herself, Imre caught a glimpse of the blonde curls of body hair dripping redly, matted and besmirched with gore. He almost vomited. Numb and disbelieving, he stared at the girl he loved, the girl he had hoped to marry, surprised in her foul blood-guilt.

'You might say we've caught her red-handed,' said Dobi.

Imre did not respond. He was still unable to grasp what he saw.

A side-door opened and Julie ran in, alerted by the noise. When she took in the tense confrontation before her, she stood hushed and anxious. Dobi grasped her hand roughly and led her out the room. He looked back at Imre and the Countess and closed the door on their shame.

Recovering, Ilona towelled her body clean of the red taint. As she did so, she cast anxious looks at Imre. Neither of them spoke. Ilona threw aside the bloodied towels and slipped into a flowing white robe. Her skin glowed with vitality. It was as smooth and white as a child's.

'Ilona?' ventured Imre. His eyes appealed for an explanation. The Countess looked at him pityingly, but said nothing. Imre gazed about the room to see what other horrors it held. He saw a black dress lying discarded on the floor. It was the dress the Countess had been wearing. A terrible new thought occurred to him.

'Where's your mother?' he demanded urgently. 'The Countess Elizabeth. Where is she?'

Ilona shook her head.

'Forget her,' said the beautiful young Countess coldly, 'She's no longer important.'

'Where is she?'

Wildly Imre stepped forward and took hold of her, pulling her robe off her shoulders. A smear of caked blood lay guiltily on her breast. He looked back to the silver vessel of blackly congealing blood. This is unbelievable, he thought. She's been bathing in the Countess's blood...

'You've killed her!' he accused. 'You've killed your own mother and you're bathing in her blood!'

It was impossible, nightmarish, yet the evidence was all about. The room reeked of blood and the charnel horrors of the battle-field returned to mock his brain.

'No. You're quite wrong.' The young Countess watched him coolly. Slowly, she approached him and took his hand in her own. He stared down at her hand.

'I am the Countess Elizabeth...' she revealed. 'The old woman you never even noticed when you came here.'

Confused, Imre stared at her. He shook his head in disbelief, rejecting the madness of her claim.

'Look at me,' she ordered, 'my face...my body...hold me...love me...'

She slipped his hand into her robe and slid it caressingly over her body, down to the core of her hot desire.

Repulsed, Imre tore his hand free and stepped back.

'No...all that blood...whose blood...?'

He felt he was going insane. His voice rose shrilly to a scream. 'Tell me! Whose?'

The Countess watched him fearfully. He was beginning to frighten her. Why was he so blind? Could he not see that she had done it all for him? For love of him?

Softly she said, 'A virgin's. No one of any importance. Just some peasant girl Dobi found.'

She saw the revulsion in his face and added quickly, 'I needed the blood for you, my darling. Don't you see? To please you...'

Imre's love for the girl was turning against him, torturing him, wrenching his heart. His mind was in turmoil, his stomach churning with nausea. Groaning, he started to back away from the foul creature he had wanted to marry.

Anxiously, she followed him and caught him in her arms, forcing him into an embrace. He struggled to free himself. She grasped his face in loving hands, forced him to look at her.

'I am Ilona,' she said. 'The one whom you love.'

Imre could smell the blood clinging to her body.

'No...don't touch me...get away!'

With a cry of disgust, he pushed her away and made for the door. She saw his intention, and, quick as a cat, reached it first. She locked the door and dropped the key into her robe pocket. Imre lunged for the key, but the Countess swerved aside and he fell against the door. Panting, defeated, he slumped against it. He no longer cared about anything, his desire to live had gone, drained away by this blood-bathing Countess.

She stood over him, her voice hard and defiant. If she could not have him by love, she would have him by force.

'Last night you tried to be unfaithful to me, but you couldn't even do that.' Her voice rose in triumph. 'You're obsessed with me!'

Wearily Imre looked up. 'Last night?' he asked.

'Yes. That whore you brought back. You think I didn't know? You think Dobi didn't tell me?'

'He's lying,' said Imre uncaring. Now he would prefer the scabbiest, vilest whore to this vampire Countess.

She laughed at his naiveté and led him by the hand to a massive oak wardrobe. Opening the door, she revealed a long line of dresses hanging from a rail. On one side were the dour black dresses of Elizabeth; on the other the light summery gowns of Ilona. Unimpressed, Imre stared at the costumes of her masquerade. Smiling grimly, the Countess stepped forward and wrenched her dresses aside with a violent motion. Behind them squatted the hunched body of Ziza.

The impact of the Countess's movement disturbed Ziza's arm and it dropped limply out of the cupboard.

Imre gasped. Ziza was naked and her skin was a bloodless blue. The red lips and rouged cheeks were in eerie contrast to the blueness of her face, giving her the appearance of a grotesque clown.

'What have you done to her?' asked Imre, horrified.

The Countess flicked the dangling arm back into the closet and shut the door on the corpse. She turned to Imre with a look of indignant innocence.

'I did nothing. You killed her,' she accused.

'Me?' Imre shook his head incredulously. He didn't know what to believe any more. Everything had the unreality of a bad dream.

'Yes,' said the Countess, sitting back in her armchair. 'And there are witnesses.'

Imre nodded ironically.

'Dobi?' he suggested.

He was beginning to see through the blackmail now, realising he was powerless in its grip.

'As many as I choose.'

She gestured for him to kneel at her feet.

'Now come and sit beside me.'

He hesitated, then complied. There was little else he could do.

'You can't escape me, my darling.' said the Countess, taking his head gently in her hands and pressing it to her lap as if he were a child. She began to stroke his untidy hair affectionately.

'My son,' she said.

Captain Balogh rode grimly through the gates of Castle Veres at the head of his black-uniformed men. Outside the main doors was a plumed funeral wagon and around it clustered a knot of curious peasants and servants, some crying. Balogh noticed them looking excitedly in his direction and talking agitatedly among themselves. Probably more superstitious nonsense about vampires, thought Balogh.

He dismounted and tethered his horse beside the funeral wagon. Leaving the Sergeant to deploy the men, he marched into the castle. He looked about and found Dobi standing at the bottom of the magnificent stairs. He joined him.

Four peasants were coming down the stairs, straining under the weight of Fabio's coffin. Their efforts were supervised by the unctuous undertaker.

Balogh shook his head sympathetically as the coffin was carried past him and out the main door. Strange, he thought, that a man who seemed so puny in life should strain the muscles of four sturdy peasants when dead.

Turning to Dobi, he asked, 'Has the Countess been told?'

The Steward nodded mournfully.

'She took it badly. Master Fabio was loved by us all,' he said, apparently genuinely upset. Balogh was surprised. He had never considered Dobi to be a friend of the old scholar.

Seeming to shake off his remorse, Dobi clapped Balogh on the back and said, 'Come, a pint of ale in Fabio's honour.'

Balogh agreed and together they strolled over to the banqueting table where a jug of beer and some mugs awaited them.

Dobi filled two mugs with the thick brew and handed one to the chief bailiff. Balogh took it appreciatively and drank a mouthful. Staring into his ale, he shook his head reflectively. 'Why did he do it?' he wondered. 'An intelligent fellow like that...'

Dobi shrugged.

'The Count's death perhaps? They were old friends.'

Balogh heaved himself into a chair.

'Yes,' he sighed. 'It's not much of a life for an old man. Not when you've seen all your friends gone and buried.'

They sat in silence for a minute, subdued by the spectre of Fabio's suicide.

'Of course there's another possibility,' suggested Dobi offhandedly. Balogh looked up as Dobi produced a pack of large cards from his belt pouch and handed them over. The Bailiff shuffled through them. They were colourful Tarot cards as used by fortune tellers.

'Fortune cards,' commented Balogh, looking up.

Dobi nodded meaningfully.

'Ah, you're thinking of the gypsy girl,' realised Balogh. 'Do you think he had something to do with her?'

'I found them in a drawer of his,' said Dobi.

'You think he killed her - then hanged himself, for remorse or guilt?'

Dobi shrugged.

'Who knows,' he said.

'What were his habits with women?' asked Balogh. 'Did he ever confide in you?'

Dobi shook his head.

'No, none of my business. But I'll tell you something. I never saw him at the Shepherd's Inn.'

Balogh guffawed. 'Maybe it would have been better if we had. At least it's healthy.' He chuckled to himself, then sniffed thoughtfully. 'Of course, he might have stumbled across the real killer who silenced him.'

He looked to Dobi for his opinion. The Steward drained his mug and put it down. He stared back at Balogh, with a sardonic smile that said the theory was beneath consideration.

'Too fanciful, eh?' mused Balogh.

Then, laughing at his suspicions, he struggled to his feet and slapped Dobi cheerfully on the back.

'Anyway, my men are searching the castle at this very moment, so we should find something,' he said, studying the Steward for his reaction.

Blankly Dobi stared back at the Bailiff, not permitting him to see anything of the fear that clutched him.

In the kitchen, the Sergeant of Bailiffs was sitting before a plate piled high with slices of juicy salami and sausage. He held his fork poised, debating which slice to start with.

Around him milled the castle's servants, frightened and chattering of the doom that had fallen upon them.

Raving lunatics, decided the Sergeant, glancing up at the commotion. He had made his decision and was chewing through a lump of spicy sausage. They were behaving as though the heathen Turks were half an hour's ride away.

Through the cluster of servants pushed the second cook, Anna, followed by her son, a fifteen year old boy, whose obesity matched that of the Sergeant. They were both wrapped in warm cloaks and laden with baggage. As Anna made for the door to the courtyard, the Sergeant stood up and caught her arm.

'And where do you think you're going?' he challenged.

'I'm not staying here. There's a curse on this place!'

She continued towards the door and the boy panted after her.

'You come back,' commanded the Sergeant. 'And your brat.' Reluctantly, the woman obeyed, herding the boy back upstairs. The Sergeant glared round the room at the other servants, who had lapsed into inquisitive silence.

'Nobody leaves without my permission. Understood?'

Resentfully, they nodded and began to whisper to one another in outraged tones.

Rosa came to the fore of the servants, dabbing at her reddened eyes with a handkerchief. Ilonka, the kitchen maid, trotted sympathetically at her heels.

'Where is she?' demanded Rosa. 'Have you found her? Have you found my little one?'

The Sergeant eyed her warily, hoping she wasn't going to erupt into one of her marathon weeping fits.

'Come on now. You mustn't give up hope,' he said reassuringly, patting her heaving shoulder with fat fingers. 'There's nothing to connect your daughter with the gypsy girl.'

Rosa was unconvinced but she turned back snivelling to join the others.

Relieved, the Sergeant sat down again and beamed at the repast before him. He raised a succulent slice towards the watering cavern of his mouth.

'Sergeant, Sergeant...over here!'

There was no mistaking the urgency in the voice of the bailiff calling him. Cursing, the Sergeant threw down his fork and jumped heavily to his feet. He paused to grab a handful of meat, crammed it between his flabby jaws and waddled off to investigate. Sensing excitement afoot, Rosa and the rest of the kitchen staff trailed behind.

The Sergeant found a shocked bailiff awaiting him at the head of the stairs to the wine cellar.

'Down here, Sergeant,' cried the bailiff and led the way down the twisting stone stairs, bearing his torch before him. The others followed, their footsteps echoing on the stone.

Emerging into the cellar, the Sergeant was confronted with rows of huge wine barrels, their squat shadows flickering blackly against the walls in the shifting glare of the torches. Rats squeaked and scattered unseen in the shadows. It was deathly cold and their breath hung like mist in the air before them. A thunderous rumble sounded as another bailiff rolled away one of the heavy barrels, revealing a dark area behind it. The bailiff swung the flaring torch nearer and what its light revealed made the servants scream with horror and fright.

Lying there, clasping each other like sleeping children, were the corpses of three naked girls, their skins strangely blue. Vivid red gashes gaped at their throats and wrists. One of the girls was young, about fifteen with an unattractive face. Another was a buxom blonde, heavily made up. The bailiff held his torch nearer, lighting the face of the third victim. Despite the work of decay and the rats, the servants easily recognised the body of Teri, the Countess's pretty chambermaid.

Rosa shrieked and, with a wail that echoed chillingly, flung herself on her knees and stretched out her hands to touch the still, cold body of her daughter. 'My baby! My Baby!' she cried over and over, rocking back and forth in her grief. Beside her, the fat Sergeant stared down, awe-struck by the gruesome discovery.

There was a chorus of screams and a thundering on the stairs as the other servants panicked and fled for the safety and warmth of the kitchen.

Balogh had issued orders for the servants to be assembled in the main hall. The male servants, who were the chief suspects, were lined up for inspection and stood like men condemned to the firing squad. Opposite them huddled the female servants. They were primarily occupied with calming Rosa. Bailiffs had been positioned at each entrance to cut down any servant attempting to escape. Between the two groups, Balogh paced thoughtfully. Nothing like this had ever happened in his district before and the Governor was going to have harsh words to say if the murderer was not quickly caught and delivered to the executioner. He decided that his actions would have to be broad and sweeping. Perhaps he would not catch the culprit instantly, but he would make sure he did not have any more opportunities to commit his filthy murders.

Dobi watched the Chief Bailiff closely. He doubted if the

pompous fool had any idea who was really responsible for the murders. Still, that quip of his about Fabio's death shielding the real killer was too close to the truth for Dobi's liking. He wondered what Balogh would do if he found out that grey-haired old Countess Elizabeth was the real villain. What could he do? The Countess was an aristocrat, a lady of the manor, and Balogh was only a petty official, a commoner. His powers were feeble compared to the Countess's powers of laissez-faire. Yet Balogh was responsible to the Governor and the Governor was directly answerable to King Matthias. Maybe he would dare take action. Even if he didn't arrest Elizabeth, he could make it very difficult for her to carry out her extravagant beauty treatment in future.

Dobi looked up and saw that the Young Countess was slowly descending the marble staircase, flanked by Imre and Julie a step behind her. He noticed that Imre's expression was blank. Probably still hasn't recovered from the shock, smiled Dobi. From her regal expression and the way she carried herself, Dobi realised that the Countess was accentuating her status, making sure that Balogh recognised her importance. Three steps from the bottom of the stairs, the young Countess stopped and motioned to the others to do likewise. Balogh really was going to have to look up to her.

Dobi strolled over to join Balogh. The bailiff was pleased to see him. Dobi appeared to him more of a friend and equal than ever before. Together they huddled like conspirators. The bailiff shook his head, attempting to convey the gravity of the situation to Dobi. 'One of them was poor Ziza,' Balogh said in a low funereal voice.

'So I've been told,' replied Dobi casually.

Balogh could not imagine a Saturday evening without pinching Ziza's plump, tender buttocks. He was about to say so, when it occurred to him that it might not be in accord with the respect normally shown to the dead. He suddenly noticed that the young Countess was surveying the scene from the stairs, presumably standing in for her ailing mother. He offered her a courteous bow and the Countess nodded back politely. She's a cool one for her age, thought Balogh. Then he turned his attention to the business at hand.

He marched over to the waiting line of male servants, Dobi following behind.

'Are they all present?' he asked, as he inspected the servants.

They looked an unlikely bunch of murderers.

Dobi nodded. 'Take your pick,' he offered helpfully.

Slowly Balogh started down the line, studying each face for signs of guilt. First in line were two ancient retainers, more dead than alive. He could hardly see them chasing young girls down the castle corridors, much as they wanted to. Then a little boot boy. He didn't look much like a precocious sex murderer...A fat pampered boy of about sixteen. Balogh scrutinised him carefully. They were a peculiar lot, fat people, thought Balogh. Particularly his Sergeant. He decided to keep the boy in mind.

Next there was a gaunt butler of middle age. The butler had a facial tic, which gave him a shifty expression. Another possible, decided Balogh. Finally, there were two exceedingly villainous characters, who looked more like brigands than valets. One was a swarthy gypsy type with a bandana round his head and the other was a stocky, surly-looking character with a huge moustache and bushy black eyebrows. Both men stared back at him insolently.

'You must have problems if you need these villains as servants,' observed Balogh.

Dobi shrugged. 'We can't pick and choose. The war claimed so many of the best,' he said.

Balogh turned back to the villainous pair. They grinned at him, considering themselves under the protection of Dobi and immune to arrest. Their arrogance angered Balogh.

'Sergeant...' he called.

The Sergeant hurried over from the main door, where he had been supervising the guard. Balogh gestured towards the suspects.

'Have these men taken to the County House for questioning,' he instructed.

The Sergeant signalled to two of the bailiffs, who stepped forward and seized the men. As they were marched away, they glared angrily at Dobi, awaiting his intervention. He turned his back on them disinterestedly.

Balogh stepped back along the line and paused before the fat boy and the butler. They were probably innocent, he thought, but it wouldn't harm to take them into preventive custody for a while.

'And these two,' commanded Balogh. Two more bailiffs advanced to apprehend the suspects. The fat boy squealed in fright as he was seized and the butler protested in disbelief. He had been in the service of the Nadasdys for thirty years and now they were letting him be dragged away like a common thief.

There was noisy consternation among the women servants as they watched their men being arrested. Shouting, Anna ran across to claim her fat son, who was, she assured the bailiffs, 'one of nature's innocents'. Dobi seized her arm as she passed and pushed her brusquely back towards the other women. The prisoners' protests died away as they were dragged out through the main door.

Balogh stared speculatively at the remaining two old men and the boot boy. They shuffled nervously under his gaze.

'The others can stay,' decided the Bailiff generously.

Relieved, the boot boy ran over into the arms of his mother, one of the scullery maids, and she hugged him happily.

Balogh turned to address the women in a loud authoritative voice.

'Right, now I want all the women, young and old, to leave the castle within the hour,' he announced.

Loud, emotional protests broke out in the ranks of the women.

Overwhelmed, Balogh held up his arms for silence.

'All right, all right. Don't panic. You'll be allowed back when this matter's cleared up. Off you go. Start packing.'

Under Dobi's amused glance, Balogh began to usher the women towards the kitchen and their quarters.

From the stairs, the young Countess addressed herself to him imperiously.

'Am I to understand this includes myself and my mother?' she asked.

'No, Countess, please forgive these unpleasant but necessary demands on your domestic staff. As for yourself, I'm sure you'll be safe with Captain Dobi and your fiancée.' He nodded, smiling towards Imre. 'But they couldn't be responsible for everyone...And it's just possible that the killer is still hiding out somewhere.'

The Countess nodded in agreement, evidently concerned.

Imre stepped past her towards Balogh, ignoring Dobi's look of warning. He wanted to make contact with Balogh, to reveal to truth to him. Balogh looked at him, but the words didn't come. He didn't know how to start, without the whole story sounding absurd.

Balogh gave him an amicable slap on the back.

'Stay close to her, lad,' he said warmly and walked away to supervise the servants.

Imre stared helplessly after him. The Countess turned to him, took his arm and led him back up the stairs like an obedient child.

An hour later, the women servants streamed out of the main gate, clutching their children and small bundles of belongings. Most of them were glad to leave, glad to be free of the castle and its curse. Some hesitated at the gate, turning to make the sign of the Evil Eye in the direction of the black tower, before picking up their baggage and continuing on their way. The two elderly retainers waved farewell.

The porcine Sergeant watched the last of the women trudge down the muddy road. Then he signalled for the portcullis to be lowered and the gates to be closed. When this was done, two bailiffs moved in and took up positions outside the gates.

Castle Veres was now isolated. Its remaining occupants were left to their own devices. And their own horrors.

Over the chessboard, Dobi and Imre faced each other. They were sitting alone in the library playing a game of chess that Imre had little interest in. A jug of wine stood next to the board and both of them were drinking heavily.

As Dobi surveyed the pieces, he chuckled throatily to himself. He was happy and not only because he was winning. There were other spheres of interest in which he was proving successful.

Imre paid neither the game nor Dobi much attention. He played passively, slumped lethargically back in his chair, his face tormented by despair. He could not shake the events of the last few days from his mind. From considering himself to be one of the most fortunate men alive, he had become a participant in a horrible ritual of blood and pain. And now there was no escape save death.

Dobi moved his bishop.

'Check,' he announced, pleased with himself, and took another sip from his drink. Imre stared sullenly at the board but made no move. Dobi leaned over and said more emphatically, 'You're in check.'

Angry frustration over his predicament gripped Imre. It made the idea of sitting down to play a civilised game like chess ridiculous. With a savage sweep of his hand he knocked the pieces from the board and stood up in disgust.

Angrily, Dobi gripped the sides of his chair, suppressing his instinct to knock Imre down. He had been winning and now he was denied the pleasure of victory. Still, let the pup have his tantrum, he thought. There were greater pleasures in the offing. And, if he was careful, Imre would help him achieve what he wanted. Composing himself, he offered Imre a conciliatory smile.

'Come on, what are you so gloomy about?' he said amicably, 'Don't you see what'll happen? She'll grow old. Cut off here, starved of little virgin girls. She'll be mine!' He laughed smugly. 'And then you can clear out. Isn't that what you want?'

Imre studied him without answering. There was truth in what the Steward said but he doubted if the future would be as casual and easy as that. The Countess was not going to timidly relinquish her beauty, or let witnesses leave the castle to tell the tale another day.

They both looked up as Julie entered, crisp and efficient in her nun-like outfit.

'The Countess wants to see you,' she said.

'Which one of us?' asked Dobi.

'You, Captain,' said Julie without emotion.

Dobi sprang up with a chuckle of appreciation. He glanced mockingly at Imre with an expression that said his words were already coming true. He swaggered out past Julie.

She did not follow him. She stood staring at Imre with a self-consciousness that was unusual for her. Perhaps his hopeless expression, like a little boy lost, appealed to her matronly sympathy. Seeing the upset chess board, she walked over to the table and stooped to pick up the pieces.

Without looking round, Imre said, quietly, accusingly, 'You knew about it from the beginning.'

She straightened up slowly without replying. Imre turned to her and saw that perhaps his words had reached her. There was just a trace of remorse in the Nanny's usually bland face.

'How could you say nothing?' he asked scornfully.

She seemed to stare before her as if seeing a nostalgic vision. He didn't think she had even heard the question. Then she spoke, in a soft caressing voice.

'I wanted her to be happy. I brought her little one into the world.'

'Ilona?' he asked. 'The real Ilona?' She did not appear to register the sarcasm in his voice. She turned to him smiling, her eyes glazed. Her hands crossed her bosom in a parody of motherly pride and Imre realised for the first time that she was not entirely sane.

'Oh, she was so beautiful,' sighed the Nanny. 'I used to tell her stories, bath her, sing her to sleep...' Her smile ebbed away into sadness.

'But then they took her from me, had to send her away, you see.'

She looked at him for understanding of her loss.

'Why didn't she come back?' asked Imre. 'They said she was on her way.' She stared wide-eyed, appalled by his ignorance.

'But didn't they tell you?' she asked. 'It was the flood that stopped her.'

Imre stared at her helplessly. Obviously the woman lived in

the past like the Countess. She seemed hardly aware of the real world. The grim dark world in which Imre was caught. He doubted whether he could make her understand his position, but it was worth a try; anything was worth trying if it meant escaping from Castle Veres. He strode up to her and rested his hands on her shoulders.

'Listen,' he said desperately. 'You know as well as I do that Captain Balogh won't find the murderer. That means we're trapped here. Trapped forever!'

She looked up at him and he saw she again had that infuriating smile with its awful smugness.

'But I'm not imprisoned. This is my home.'

He stared at her smiling face for a moment, then turned away in despair.

When Dobi entered her room, the radiant, beautiful young Countess threw her arms around him and began teasing him with soft kisses. He tried to conceal his enjoyment, eyed her knowingly.

'What do you want from me?' he asked.

She pouted briefly with annoyance and resumed her display of affection, stroking his lips, kissing his nose and mouth. Coldly, he waited for her request.

Finally, she stepped back and hung her head unhappily. 'I shan't go to sleep tonight,' she said, 'knowing it can happen any time.'

She looked up, her eyes appealing.

'We must have someone in the castle. Ready.'

Dobi snorted with disdain.

'How am I supposed to get her past the bailiffs?'

She threw her arms about him and held him close.

'You can outwit them, you know you can,' she said beguilingly.

Dobi sighed to himself. It was difficult to resist her coquetry when she was so beautiful. And besides, there was a way...He had thought the idea over and found it flawless in every respect.

'Very well,' he said.

Firmly, he loosened her grip and stepped aside. He did not want her to think he was completely under her control.

'You'll bring her tonight?' asked the Countess enthusiastically.

His smile was reassuring.

'She'll be here when you need her.'

'In that case,' said the Countess playfully, tilting her head to one side. 'I shall be here when you need me.'

Dobi looked her soft young body up and down and began to chuckle in a way she did not find at all pleasant.

Clouds hid the moon and the sky was as black as a velvet cape. The two bailiffs guarding the main gate paced side by side to keep warm, and counted the minutes to the end of their shift. Deriding Captain Balogh, they decided that the murderer had fled long ago and that their uncomfortable presence was pointless. They would have thought it even more pointless had they seen Dobi entering the castle through a secret door at the back, accompanied by a young girl.

She was heavily cloaked and a hood hid her face. In silence, Dobi led her through the blackness of the courtyard and into the forbidding castle. Snatching a torch from the wall, he guided her up the servants' stairs to a small room at the top. The room Teri had lived in.

He opened the door and bundled her ungraciously inside.

'Remember, not a sound now,' he cautioned and swung the door shut, plunging the small room into darkness. Outside, he slammed the bolt and hoped that the sound of her sobs would not be noticed.

The Countess sat up in bed watching Julie poke the dying embers of the fire. Beside her, Imre lay with his head on the pillow, eyes closed in a semblance of sleep. He was not asleep but he hoped, without much faith, that his appearance might dissuade the Countess from forcing him to do her bidding once Julie had left the room. It seemed incredible that the act which had given him so much joy a few days previously now seemed a vile ordeal.

The Countess was worried. She did not know how long her youth and beauty would last and, with the passing of each minute, she became more agitated. The vision of turning into a loathsome hag, while held in Imre's loving embrace, haunted her.

'Goodnight, Countess,' said the nanny, making for the door to her room.

'Wait a moment, Julie,' said the Countess, slipping out of bed and running across to the old woman. She draped an arm around her and led Julie to the bedroom door.

'Captain Dobi has promised to go to the village and bring me a girl. But I fear he may have betrayed me. He is jealous, you see,' she said pointedly, looking at Imre's sleeping form.

'Jealous of my beauty and of my love for Imre.'

'What do you want me to do?' asked Julie, mystified.

The Countess held her with an imploring look.

'Search the castle...every room. If you find her, don't disturb her. Just come back and tell me to put my mind at rest. Go now, please hurry.'

She hugged and kissed her and the nanny left the room.

The Countess turned and looked back at Imre.

'Wake up, Sleepyhead,' she said. 'I'm coming for you...'

In the corridor, Julie took a torch down from a wall-bracket and shuffled over to Ilona's old room. Opening the door, she held the torch inside and briefly surveyed the empty room. Disappointedly, she shut the door and moved across towards the library.

'Looking for somebody?' a jeering voice behind her demanded. Her heart leaping, she turned to see Dobi lounging against the wall of the corridor by the servants' quarters. A mug of ale was clutched in his hand and he swayed drunkenly. Something in his manner frightened her and she quickly began an explanation.

'The Countess is anxious -'

Dobi interrupted with a flick of his hand.

'Tell her the girl is here. She's ready...' he laughed unpleasantly, '...like a turkey waiting for Christmas.'

Laughing at a private joke, he swaggered unsteadily towards her. As he passed, he held up his mug of ale in a taunting salute.

'Goodnight, Julie. Have wet dreams...'

Laughing, he rounded the corner to his own room. Holding her breath, Julie waited until she heard the slam of his door. There had been something especially nasty in the way he had looked at her and she felt sure it was something to do with the girl. As quickly as she could, she directed her tired legs towards the servants' quarters.

At the bottom of the servants' stairs, Julie stopped and listened intently. It seemed to her that she had heard a low murmuring...No sound reached her except the crackling of the torch. Shaking her head, she turned to go, unwilling to climb the long stairs on a fruitless errand. Then, she heard it again, quite unmistakably this time. The sound of someone crying.

Slowly, the old nanny began to climb the stairs. As she climbed nearer to Teri's room, the crying grew louder. She could see by the harsh light of the torch that a wooden bolt had been placed across the door. It had not been there the previous day.

With difficulty, she heaved aside the bolt and opened the door on the blackness inside. Holding up the torch, she saw the figure of a young girl jump up startled and back away. There was something familiar about the action, something that made her thrust the torch nearer to the girl and cry out in recognition.

'Ilona!' she gasped.

Afraid, the girl stared back with wide, blue eyes. Then her expression softened and tears of relief clouded her eyes.

'Nanny? Is it you, Nanny?'

Julie closed her eyes as if struck with grief.

'Oh, my little one,' she moaned.

Ilona edged nearer.

'You remember me?'

Laying the torch down, Julie took her eagerly in her arms and hugged her.

'Oh, yes...Yes!...I remember you, my child...my baby...'

In the Nanny's arms, Ilona felt protected for the first time in days. Tears streaming down her face, she held the old woman tightly, exactly as she had done as a child with a hurt to confide.

'Oh, Nanny, please help me,' she pleaded.

'My father's dead...I haven't seen my mother...I don't know what's happening to me.'

She shuddered in Julie's arms.

'Shush, my little one...' comforted Julie. 'You must be patient...'

Gently, she stroked the weeping girl's hair and, almost imperceptibly, she began to hum a lullaby.

It was the morning of her wedding to Imre and the Countess was in excellent spirits as she presided over the breakfast table.

Her wit had not shown itself so brightly since the evening of her 'arrival'.

Her breakfast companions did not appear to share her enthusiasm, however. Dobi made his disapproval known by well-timed, cynical comments on the marriage preparations. Imre, who had no more reason to be enthusiastic than Dobi, picked sullenly at his food and did not look up once at his intended bride. Even Julie displayed more reserve than usual, a fact which the Countess attributed to some kind of matronly resentment at the marriage.

At the back of the main hall, two bailiffs, kindly loaned by Captain Balogh, were busy hanging up long-garlanded decorations. The Castle had not seen such colour since the great balls of the Countess's youth.

As one of the remaining servants cleared away the plates, the Countess chose an apple and bit into it. She looked at Imre with amusement and addressed him between mouthfuls.

'They say it's an ill omen...for us to see each other on the morning of our wedding.'

She smiled sceptically.

'But I'm not superstitious. Are you, darling?'

Imre did not humour her with a reply. Without showing annoyance, the Countess put aside the remains of her apple and stood up. She gave Julie an extra big hug for such an important morning and headed towards the family chapel. Wordlessly, Dobi flung down his napkin and followed after her.

Imre remained seated. He was aware that Julie was staring intently towards him and it annoyed him. But he did not care to return to his own room and the lonely silence of his own company.

The Countess passed under the high-peaked archway and entered the family chapel. Two small choir boys in black and white robes were keenly laying out the altar cloth in preparation for the afternoon's ceremony. The Countess clasped her hands delightedly and laughed.

She turned to Dobi as he walked up beside her. 'I'm so happy,' she confided. The choir boys giggled nervously at being watched by such an important person and began to arrange baskets of flowers.

'Dobi, I have decided to overrule Captain Balogh's orders, just for today,' said the Countess.

'I want everyone to share my happiness and attend the ceremony.'

Before Dobi could question the wisdom of such a decision, the Countess turned with a flurry of her blue velvet dress and re-entered the main hall. He followed quickly behind. 'All the female servants and trades people are invited.' She paused beside the two bailiffs who were draping the hall with bright hangings.

'Even our friendly bailiffs are welcome,' she said pointedly. 'And there must be free drink for everybody.'

The bailiffs smiled and bowed in recognition of her generosity.

Turning to Dobi, the Countess said, 'Will you make the arrangements, please?'

Dobi turned his back on the bailiffs and eyed the Countess slyly.

'And what of your mother? Will she be attending?' he casually asked.

The Countess gave him a hateful look of rebuke but, seeing the bailiffs watching her, she was forced to smile graciously.

'Sadly, no. She is really quite ill today.'

The bailiffs shook their heads sympathetically at the distress in the young girl's voice.

'I'm most concerned,' she added, sighing, and moved away to the breakfast table. Heartened by their sight of the beautiful bride, the bailiffs resumed their work. Dobi strode back to his room.

The Countess hovered around Julie who began to butter another slice of bread, apparently anxious to stay at the table.

'When you're finished, Julie, will you help me with the wedding dress?' asked the Countess impatiently, wishing the nanny would hurry.

'Yes, Countess,' promised Julie, making no visible sign to hurry her meal.

Stopping briefly to blow a kiss towards Imre, the Countess danced lightly across the hall and up the stairs. Imre snorted contemptuously at this display of bridal bliss and resumed his apathetic slouch across the table.

When the Countess was out of sight, Julie leaned over urgently and grasped his hand.

Surprised, he looked up.

'Master Imre, will you please come with me. There's someone you have to meet,' she said.

Imre hesitated. The horse-faced woman had been anything but a friend until now. Yet there was a desperation in her appeal that made it difficult to ignore.

Already Julie was halfway across the hall. She turned and beckoned, imploring him not to delay. Hastily, Imre sprang up and followed her towards the kitchens and the servants' quarters.

Still puzzled, but anxious to lend support to any act that would prevent his marriage to the Countess, Imre followed the nanny up the servants' stairs. They were in a dark, evil-smelling part of the castle that Imre had not visited before. Apprehensively, he wondered if the nanny was about to show him more evidence of the Countess's cruelty - disembowelled children, or corpses bearing the red marks of torture...

At the top of the stairs, the nanny halted before a barred door. With eager fingers she unbolted it and led him inside.

Imre stopped, startled by the sight of a lovely young girl, brushing her hair. Her surprise was no less and, crying out, she turned anxiously to Julie for reassurance.

'Don't' be afraid, my dear,' said the Nanny. 'This is Imre Toth. He is a guest in the castle.'

Turning to Imre, she informed him, 'This is Countess Ilona. The Ilona that cried in my arms as a babe.'

Masking his surprise, Imre accepted the hand that Ilona offered and kissed it gently. In her own way, Ilona was almost as beautiful as her rejuvenated mother. She had ringlets of soft brown hair, an attractive little nose and blue eyes which showed pleasure at meeting him, but could not hide her sorrow. As they looked at one another, there was an immediate rapport. They recognised in each other fellow victims ensnared by the same spreading web of terror. Under different circumstances, Imre would have been delighted to meet such an attractive girl. But within the grim walls of Castle Veres, the sight of this innocent, beautiful creature only added to the torment in Imre's soul.

Ilona frowned, trying to remember something. 'Your name is familiar to me,' she said, unable to recall where she had heard it.

'My father was General Toth.'

Ilona's face brightened in recognition.

'Of course! My father spoke of him in letters. His best friend.'

She blushed and lowered her eyes.

'He also spoke of you,' she said in such a sweet way that Imre felt a sharp pain of regret and wished he had met her without ever having heard of Castle Veres.

'I believe it was his wish that we should someday meet,' he sighed.

Julie had been watching this sad encounter from the doorway, ready to give warning if anyone approached. Now she heard the Countess's voice calling her anxiously from afar.

'Oh Master Imre!' she said in alarm. 'We cannot stay or we will be discovered.'

Despairing, she began to tug him towards the door.

'Who is it?' asked Ilona, wide-eyed, sensing the nanny's fear.

Imre hesitated, unwilling to leave the frightened girl. Again Julie tugged at his arm.

'Come quickly,' she pleaded.

'I'll come back later,' Imre promised Ilona.

Reluctantly, he followed Julie outside and watched the nanny replace the bolt.

Wiping her hands, she turned to him, resentment making her face hard.

'Dobi brought her here because of her virgin's blood. We have to help her to escape,' she whispered.

Together, they started down the stairs. Imre's mind was reeling. For days he had let apathy and resignation overcome him. His position seemed hopeless, his defeat assured. But now, someone else's life was in peril. Her safety depended on him and he had to act fast.

The urgency of Ilona's plight stimulated Imre. His thoughts came fast and, out of his excitement, a plan began to take shape.

'Wait,' he said as they reached the bottom of the stairs. Julie paused, responding to the determination in his voice.

'Listen...you must lead her away during the ceremony. No one will notice your absence in the crowd. Take her out to the stables.'

He spoke with the cool authority that had made him one of Hungary's youngest officers.

'Will you meet us there?' asked Julie.

Imre shook his head regretfully.

'I cannot.'

'But Master Imre -' pleaded Julie, her face desperate.

'You know I cannot,' he insisted.

He paused with quiet despair and for the first time he became aware of church bells joyfully celebrating the Countess's wedding day.

'God knows I wish to leave with her,' he said resignedly. 'But I have witnessed so much blood...my very being reeks to heaven with it.'

Julie held his arm comfortingly.

'But Master Imre, you are innocent. As innocent as Ilona is. You must go together.'

'Together?' he repeated cynically. 'It cannot be.'

'Julie...I'm waiting!'

The angry voice of the Countess sounded much nearer now. Julie looked up in fright.

'Take her,' she urged, with final desperation.

'And raise false hopes...to break them later?'

Imre shook his head resolutely. 'No, it's unthinkable. You must save her.'

He pushed her away, exhorting her to leave.

'Go now, quickly, before we are discovered.'

With a last despairing look at him, Julie hurried away down the corridor to find her mistress. Imre slumped against the wall, feeling suddenly drained after the burst of energy that had gripped him. The church bells rang mockingly in his ears, laughing at his despondency.

Slowly, he turned and stared up the stairs towards Ilona's door. He felt reluctant to leave without a farewell or some word of encouragement. He felt as drawn to her as he had once been to her mother. Heavily, he began to mount the stairs to her room.

Ilona ran to him as he entered, relieved to see him and not Dobi.

'Oh, please tell me what is happening,' she implored.

She began to tease a curl of her hair nervously between her fingers. 'Foolish nanny says I should be patient. But how can I? She tells me nothing!'

Imre stared at the agitated young girl. She was still so young, so innocent, more suited to a convent than to this castle of horrors.

'She is so stubborn, she makes me quite angry at times,' fumed Ilona, flaring her pretty nostrils.

'Countess Ilona, your life is in danger,' said Imre brutally before she could continue her tirade.

Shocked she turned to him.

'From whom?'

'I cannot say, but trust me. You must leave at once.'

'Leave my home?' She was bewildered, incredulous. 'There's so much I have to do. I want to see my father's grave and my mother...' Her voice softened. 'I must speak with her.'

Imre watched her with helpless pity. 'It's impossible.'

'Why?' she demanded. 'Tell me what there is to fear.'

'Please, I beg you, do not argue.' said Imre firmly. 'In a short while, Julie will take you to the stables. Talk to no one.'

She threw back her head sulkily. 'I will say I am the Countess Ilona.'

'No, you will not be believed,' he said harshly. 'Take a horse and ride with haste to the County House. Wait there for Captain Balogh and tell him your misfortunes.'

'Will you not come with me?' Her blue eyes were pleading. 'I fear to go alone after what has happened to me.'

'You must not fear,' said Imre, knowing he was asking her to find courage he was not sure he possessed himself.

'Please come with me!' she begged.

Her attractive face was so stricken with foreboding and grief that Imre felt torn with indecision. Finally, he said, 'Very well. I'll meet you at the stables.'

Her face brightened immediately. 'You will not fail me?' she asked with an anxious smile.

'No,' he said, hoping to die rather than break his promise.

She smiled happily and he obeyed an impulse to snatch her hand and kiss it. She put her arms around him in an innocent embrace and for several seconds, their young bodies were held together tightly. Her tenderness was so pure that Imre was sickened to recall Elizabeth's worldly caresses.

'I must leave you now,' he said, reluctantly ending their warm embrace.

'Do everything that Julie tells you,' he said from the doorway.

'I will. I promise.'

Then he closed the door and hurried away to prepare for his marriage to her mother.

The tolling of the church bells spread a cheer through the land which made the peasants think of Carnival Day and the great holy festivals. There was laughter in the fields as flasks of cider and potent schnapps were passed from hand to hand and voices were raised in joyful singing. Even when the mighty bell of the Castle's black tower added its sober resonance, the workers' spirits were not dulled.

Towards the Castle a steady stream of guests made their way, on foot or in droshkys. There was black-clad Rosa and her coterie of kitchen staff; proud tradesmen and their families; stout yeomen and off-duty bailiffs. They strutted before the eyes of their uninvited fellows, all wearing their finest clothes. The women wore frilly white blouses, gaily embroidered, and black flaring skirts, and the men wore colourful sashes over their leather breeches.

Under the gaze of the Sergeant of Bailiffs, the wedding guests filed under the portcullis into the castle. He scrutinised each festive face, searching for tell-tale signs of the blood-hungry vampire.

The only person to avoid his suspicion was the Bishop of Csjthe who was to conduct the wedding ceremony. He arrived in a black two-wheeled carriage, fervently bestowing blessings on the stragglers as he passed.

When all the guests were within the castle, the Sergeant barked orders for the portcullis to be lowered and he and his men went to investigate the free food and wine.

The family chapel of the Nadasdys was brightly arrayed with the reds and yellows of summer blooms hanging from the walls. A shaft of sunlight flamed through the stained-glass window of Abraham and struck golden the upright crucifix on the altar.

The Bishop solemnly entered in his flowing black and white robes and jewel-encrusted mitre, and ascended the altar. Two choir-boys hastened to finish lighting the multitude of white candles as the chapel filled with quietly talking guests.

Imre and Balogh slowly made their way through the congregation towards their place before the altar. Both wore their best ceremonial uniforms and displayed a sleek military elegance that won comments from the ladies. As Imre pressed forward, he was only half aware of the hearty hands slapping his back and the strangers pushing their red, drink-reeking faces towards his to mumble platitudes and congratulations. He maintained a small modest smile on his lips but the laughing faces and their comments were as remote as a dream. His actual thoughts were on Ilona who would soon be waiting for him at the stable.

He and Balogh took up positions before the altar. The Bishop turned and nodded gravely towards them. At the same time a low hush fell upon the congregation and the Bishop looked out into the hall.

Looking extraordinarily beautiful, the young Countess appeared at the top of the staircase. She wore a red and white gown, sparkling with pearls, that was both virginal and alluring. A crown, as golden as her hair, rested upon her head and a white veil covered her perfect features.

To her right stood Dobi, an imposing figure in his handsome black uniform. She waited until all eyes were upon her. Then she accepted Dobi's arm and, together, they began to descend the staircase with slow measured steps. Behind them came Julie carrying the Countess's white train.

Imre watched her as she approached. She was more beautiful today than he had ever seen her. He was the envy of every man present. Yet the sight of her hard-bought beauty gave him only a feeling of sickly bitterness.

Majestically, the Countess glided through the awe-struck congregation, acknowledging well-wishers with a regal smile, enjoying the whispers of admiration. No empress could have made a more splendid impression as she moved up the aisle and took her place beside Imre.

Imre hardly spared her a glance as she stood next to him. He turned to Julie and gave her a look that was imperceptible to the others but which she readily understood. Unnoticed, she disappeared into the congregation and, moments later, left the back of the aisle and hurried towards the servants' quarters.

Imre turned back to face the Bishop without a glance at his resplendent bride. She, however, stared at him with doting eyes from beneath her veil. Her infatuation charmed the congregation who responded with delighted whispers.

The whispering ceased as the Bishop smiled benevolently at the young couple before him and began to intone the melodious Latin verses of the wedding ceremony.

As they emerged from Teri's room, Julie draped a warm cloak around Ilona's shoulders. Furtively, they began to move down the stairs.

Ilona was nervous but her nervousness was that of excitement, not the cold fear that Julie knew. The girl was fascinated by the romantic intrigue that surrounded her. It was almost as exciting as the events which always befell a young girl in a minstrel's love-song. With all her heart, she longed to know the truth behind her imprisonment and the Castle's hinted-at mysteries.

Cautiously, Julie led her to the first landing. Seen in the daylight, the surroundings seemed far less foreboding to Ilona. She recognised where she was - except that everything seemed much smaller than she remembered. The sight stirred happy memories of childhood and she felt that she was at last emerging from a bad dream.

It was then that Ilona heard the faint sounds of the Bishop's liturgy. She stood still and listened, straining to make sense of the distant words. Julie was half-way down the next flight of stairs before she realised Ilona was no longer behind her. She looked back.

'Come, child. Hurry!' she urged.

The girl remained transfixed, listening intently.

'No, listen, Nanny...I can hear a priest.'

She looked down at Julie.

'What's happening?' she demanded. 'Is it my father's funeral?'

'It's no concern of yours,' said Julie, as she ran up and began to tug the girl's arm.

'Quickly, we must hurry!'

Ilona shook her off, irritably.

'No, leave me. I want to know. I must know!'

The words were a command; she had assumed the authority of her rank.

Close to tears with helplessness, Julie watched the head-strong girl run off in the direction of the ceremony. As quickly as her tired legs would carry her, she followed.

Ilona ran to the top of the staircase and hid in the shadows. Below, she could see a congregation of well-dressed people and, before them, a young couple kneeling at the feet of a Bishop. She felt a thrill of excitement as she realised she was watching a wedding ceremony and that the groom was Imre Toth, the gallant soldier she had spoken to.

It was so puzzling, she thought. Why had he warned her against a terrible danger when here he was, calmly getting married? And what would his bride think if she knew that her new husband had pledged a secret tryst with another girl, right after his marriage? Ilona felt painfully jealous as she looked towards the bride. She could not see the girl's face because it was averted, but she was certain it must be very beautiful for Imre to want to marry her. She suddenly experienced a pang of guilt at the romantic hopes she had held about him.

Beside her, Julie arrived, breathless from her pursuit. The nanny pulled her sleeve, wordlessly pleading for them to leave. Ilona angrily resisted. The ceremony was coming to a climax and she wanted to watch.

Imre took the dazzling ring from Captain Balogh's hand. The stone was a priceless diamond, the prize of the Countess's collection. Indifferently, he slipped it onto his bride's finger. He glanced at her bowed head. Soon, he would be free of her and her hideous castle.

He would be riding through the green forest, sharing the pure taste of freedom with the sweet Ilona.

Above them, the Bishop was intoning the last blessing. As he raised his hand to make the Sign of the Cross and seal the union with God's approval, the Countess lifted her head and looked straight at him.

The Bishop's voice faltered, his arm was paralysed in its descent. At his feet, instead of the radiant young bride he expected, squatted an obscenely ugly old woman, leering up at him in a parody of happiness. The Bishop gasped with horror and grasped the heavy crucifix with both hands, calling upon God to protect him from Satan's wiles.

With a shriek of grief, the Countess leapt to her feet and looked despairingly about her. The guests saw a grimacing hag standing in the bridal garments worn seconds before by a beautiful young girl. At the sight of the terrifying transformation, they screamed in horror and amazement, certain they were witnessing a visitation of the Devil. Their surprise lasted only a second before panic broke out and they fought and trampled each other to escape from the presence of Evil.

The Countess knew immediately what had happened and what needed to be done. She turned to Dobi and snatched his dagger from its sheath before he could stop her.

Weakly, Dobi stared at her. He knew it was all over for them. Their secret was revealed and they would be punished for their sins as he had known all along. There was no longer any escape. Unless it was the escape the Countess had chosen - into madness.

Turning from Dobi with disgust, the Countess pushed past Imre and an incredulous Chief Bailiff and plunged into the crowd, holding the gleaming dagger above her head. The guests scattered before her, terrified by her menacing blade, her banshee-scream and - her face.

'Where is she?' howled the Countess.

Berserk, she cut her way through the screaming confusion, hacking down those who did not move out of her way fast enough. Only one thing mattered to her insane mind - find the virgin and wallow in her blood. Then the ceremony could resume and she would marry Imre. And they would be happy ever after, just like in the stories Nanny used to tell her when she was a little girl...

As the Countess rushed past, Rosa, the cook, threw out a panicked hand and tore the Countess's veil from her face. The full horror of hanging, decayed flesh was revealed, and more screams echoed in the hall. The maddened Countess slashed at Rosa's face and ran on, heading for the servants' quarters and the refreshing blood that awaited her.

Glancing up, Imre saw what the Countess had not yet seen - Julie and Ilona huddled at the top of the stairs. Even as he saw them and fear gripped his throat, the Countess changed direction and headed, unchallenged, towards the stairs. Imre plunged into the turmoil, desperate to reach Ilona before the Countess.

The Countess cackled at the sight of Julie and the girl at the head of the stairs. Good old faithful Julie, she thought. The nanny had seen her mistress' distress and hurried to find the remedy.

Triumphantly brandishing the dagger, she started up the stairs towards her salvation.

As the Countess approached, Julie shrank whimpering into the shadows, powerless to prevent the confrontation between mother and daughter. Ilona watched the wild figure running up the stairs towards her with as much curiosity as fear. There was something oddly familiar about the features of the deranged woman. The figure came nearer and then Ilona was sure she knew who it was.

Horrified, she descended a couple of steps.

'Mother?' she whispered uncertainly.

The Countess stopped and her knife-hand wavered. She examined the sobbing girl in front of her. The blue eyes...the pert nose...the brown ringlets. Of course! It was her daughter, Ilona. The Countess's face softened, a smile crept across her pitted face.

Ilona! Her own lovely daughter, home at last.

Suddenly, the Countess's lips sprang back over yellowed teeth in a terrible animal snarl. Ilona? How could that be? She was Ilona! This must be some impostor come to steal Imre from her.

Screaming with rage and anguish, the Countess raised the dagger and lunged at Ilona.

'Don't touch her!' Imre shouted as he bounded up the steps behind the Countess. Seeing he was too late, he flung himself across the few remaining steps.

The dagger was falling to slash Ilona's neck when Imre seized the Countess's arm and deflected the blow. Losing her balance, the Countess fell heavily against her lover. Imre grunted as he felt the burning pain of the dagger stabbing into his stomach. He looked down at the wound and almost laughed at the irony. He, who had been so revolted by the sight of blood, was now watching his own spill away down the stairs.

Ilona screamed as Imre sagged to his knees, gushing blood. She reached out her hand to him and he looked up. For one agonised, tantalising moment, their eyes met and each knew the other was thinking of what might have been.

Then he fell back and toppled heavily down the stairs and came to rest below. Balogh and the few remaining celebrants looked on in frozen horror.

At the head of the stairs, the Countess looked down at his body, hardly comprehending what she had done. The dagger slipped from her numbed hand and clattered on the steps. Slowly, the realisation came that she had destroyed the only thing she still loved. Tears began to stream down her haggard face and mixed with Imre's blood on the stone steps.

Her mind helped her grief by pushing all her memories, all her recollections of the recent horrors into a dark recess. As her awareness dwindled to a distant silence, the Countess slumped tiredly onto the steps. She felt so weary. She really should not rush about so at her age, she thought.

The Countess stared down at the dark splash of Imre's blood and wondered why her emotions were aroused at the sight. What significance could it ever have held for her?

The dungeon of Castle Veres was dark and airless and the floor was covered with filthy straw. In the straw lay Dobi and Julie, their heads bowed. They rarely looked up, being weighed down by guilt and by massive rustling chains that gripped their legs, arms and necks.

The Countess sat motionless beneath the tiny grille that the jailers jokingly referred to as a window. Her eyes were dull and staring and only the slow rhythm of her breathing indicated that she was alive.

Of her legendary beauty, no trace remained. The creased desiccated skin of her face hung in decayed tatters and the whole of her body was stricken with yellow-tipped pustules oozing wetly. The shoulder-length hair was now grey and matted. Her limbs were skeletal and so withered that she seemed only half her former size.

From outside came the sound of an approaching carriage. A meagre gleam of awareness showed itself in the Countess's eyes as, with infinite slowness, she forced herself up on trembling legs and looked out through the narrow bars. It must be some noble visitor from afar, come to visit her, she thought.

The approach road to the Castle was lined with excited villagers. Their mood was festive yet there was an unpleasant maliciousness in their delight. The object of the excitement was slowly approaching in a black open carriage. As he drew nearer, the villagers raised hoarse cheers or muttered direly among themselves.

He was a tall, thin man, completely dressed in black with a hood covering his head. Through the narrow eye-slits he peered out at his admirers. He was the Public Executioner and on his lap lay the black box containing the rope that would hang the blood-bathing Countess.

Maryska watched the hangman pass with cruel pleasure. She turned away and tottered towards the Castle. Her belly was huge with child. It was Grigory's child she claimed, though some doubted it. His sons, Sergei and Georgy, had recently fallen victims to the plague, but her man's blood would live on in the new child.

She stood beneath the dark dungeon window and shook her fist towards it. Curses and abuse sprang from her lips although she could not see if there was anyone to hear her anger.

In the cell, the Countess stared glassily out through the grille. Below, she could see a woman who seemed to be shouting up at her. Maybe she was shouting a greeting, hoped the Countess. She struggled to make out the words. Yes, the woman was speaking to her. She could hear her name being called out.

Her anger exhausted, Maryska hurried away to rejoin the celebration. The Countess watched her go, then turned from the bars and sank back down onto the soiled straw, pleased that her faithful villagers had not forgotten her.

She liked her name. It had a noble sound to it and she repeated it aloud to herself in the darkness - 'COUNTESS DRACULA!'

COUNTESS DRACULA

QUEEN OF BLOOD

LIMITED EDITION OF 5,000 CARD SET — 11 COLOUR GORE SOAKED IMAGES.

Each set contains 11 *full colour* photographs (140mm x 200mm) of blood drenched wenches and the wicked Countess. These original and exclusive cards are based on interpretations of scenes contained in the book *Countess Dracula* by Michel Parry, published by Redemption Books.

Concept / Art Direction — Nigel Wingrove
Photography — Chris Bell
Stylist — Spencer Horne
Hair and Make up — Ashley Mae
Models:
Countess Dracula — Eileen Daly
Gypsy Women— Maria
Peasant Women— Marie Harper

© REDEMPTION FILMS 1995